Looking for Sea Turtles

Andy Gabriel-Powell

Copyright © 2018 Andy Gabriel-Powell

ISBN-13: 9781980622840
ISBN-10: 1980622841

Cover design by: Mike Weston
Library of Congress Control Number: 2018675309
Printed in the United States of America

For Jenn

Love

"Love is never found. It finds us. We are its prey. We will ourselves to be caught, helpless in its rapture. To be enslaved and to do all that it takes to remain there, no matter the heartache, the pain, the gamble, the cost. For to be in Love, is everything. To Love's own pleasure, we are but toys, to play with, so long as we are willing, and able, to be all that it wants us to be. We long for the fire Love brings. We dare it to flare so bright, so uncontrollable, so undeniable, each and every time we gaze upon the one we are joined with in Loves embrace. For some, the fire never truly breathes, the embers, cold for ever too soon after life betrothed has begun. For others, Love is a rite of passage, a task, an expectation, a chore. Yet, for the chosen few, Love leaves them entwined forever, a forgotten quest in its search for others to play its heart-breaking game."
ANDY GABRIEL-POWELL

Beginnings

I am the Celt.

I first met Jenn one sunny Sunday afternoon in the late of May 2012. We were on Hatteras island, off the coast of North Carolina. My purpose for being there, to research for a book about a colony of Englishmen and women that had been lost more than four hundred years ago. Well, that was the plan anyway...

Jenn arrived with our Project Archaeologist. It was her reward he said, for defending her dissertation. She was to be our field supervisor.

She walked into the room with eyes nervous wide, flicked her hair as though to brush aside those nerves, and sat down to the introductions. She was wearing tie-dye, and she was an impossible dream... Tall, high-waisted, stunning, and yet oblivious to just how beautiful she was. There was not a hint of make-up, or blemish on her skin. She flicked her long sun-bleached hair once more, and smiled.

When I think back to that moment now, I realise there was something in that smile; a broad grin, a slight flush of the cheeks, bright blue, almost innocent, yet deeply knowing eyes. I could not help but take an instant liking to her, despite believing I could never reach her.

Introductions were simple enough, but I was an insecure man and made the usual hash such a man does in these situations. I know now that Jenn saw through me in an instant.

In the hours that followed there was no hint of what was to come, we merely planned the following day's activities, ate, talked, drank bourbon, and talked some more. Conversation was easy with Jenn; the questions came thick and fast, and I was all too willing to respond to this beautiful creature, if only to keep her from wandering off.

The following morning found us burdened with the task of loading the vehicles in preparation for the day's activities.
Being the chivalrous type, or perhaps just trying to be macho, I volunteered to carry the heavier burdens to the truck. Jenn though, was having none of it. She grabbed the largest box and manfully threw it in the back of the truck, perhaps; I thought, as a gesture of feminist defiance, perhaps even as a warning shot that this woman was of her own making.
I liked her spirit.

We were organised into small teams that day and set to task among the heavy undergrowth.
I set out alone, but it was not long before that wondrous creature I had been stifling my pointless dreams at, chose to join me.
It was a strange time; for together we worked as though only the best teams ever do, seamlessly. It was as though we had always worked together; somewhere, sometime past; each knowing the drill, each knowing how to support the other in our onerous task, onerous, not least, for knowing that the undergrowth we ploughed our way through was infested with ticks, a hideous invention of Mother Earth and one which I thoroughly detest. Apparently, so did Jenn; for when one of them, the largest of their kind, determined it would crawl across her carefully detailed field notes, she flicked it onto a nearby tree-stump with the most abrupt of profanities and disgust. I offered her my axe, thinking she would use the butt side of it to flatten said tick, but no. Snatching the axe from my hand, she swung at the tick, blade down, and cleaved the tick perfectly in two.

As she stood there wide-eyed, and stunned by her accuracy, the laughter exploded inside me in a way I had not felt before. At that moment, I wanted to pick her up, squeeze her, swing her around me, in part for celebration, but mostly, I confess, for giving me the first release from my tortured soul since I did not know when.

As the evening's glorious sunset beckoned several of us onto the balcony of our lodgings, I was only too happy to see Jenn among them.

Gradually, and with some satisfaction, we worked our way through another bottle of bourbon. As we did, so the conversation became easier. Jenn, as ever, showed a confidence I could only admire, while I, as ever, struggled with my efforts to be entertaining.

Eventually, I learned to shut up, and spent the remainder of the evening happily following Jenn around like an ever obedient puppy, grateful for even the smallest tid-bit acknowledgment of my existence.

That night, I slept with deep but satisfying emotions. I had enjoyed several undivided hours of companionship with a beautiful, intelligent woman; several hours longer than the fleeting moment my life probably deserved. I had also learned to laugh again, albeit with an excess known only to those who experience the sudden release of emotions years long pent.

It was late the following day that it became evident I was suffering from a serious outbreak of mosquito bites, for which, our nursing colleague offered a cream to ease my discomfort.

Jokingly I offered the cream to the females of our party in the hope that one of them would take pity on this irksome male in need of some self-gratification. To my delight, Jenn volunteered. As her fingers dabbed the cream upon each wheal on my skin, the euphoria within carried my soul away once more.

It may have been perhaps a day or two later that the feeling inside, fueled by the near constant presence of Jenn, erupted in the rashest of ways.

As we found ourselves journeying home together, alone for at least the third time that week, I found myself gambling my new found happiness, and in the most profound of ways. Was I about to destroy what could be a simple, happy, couple of weeks... the first in my life for so long, or was there an opportunity to secure the undivided attention of this gorgeous, intelligent creature for a little longer, if only for a simple, platonic, evening..?

As humiliation beckoned, I asked Jenn whether she would like to go out for a meal that night.

I cannot tell you how crazy it felt to ask her. She was twenty years younger than me and I could find twenty reasons for her to think I was being offensive, perhaps even lecherous.

As I made the saddest attempt to sound apologetic for blurting out my question, all the while thinking how I could negotiate my way out of this madness, Jenn interrupted me with a simple: "Yes".

Arriving back at our shared lodgings, there was no easy way to explain why we were not joining our colleagues for dinner that night - so we avoided the risk.

As though fate had chosen to help us, the bedrooms in the lodgings were below the living quarters. This made it easy for us to sneak into our respective rooms, shower, change, and leave without notice or challenge from awkward questions. I felt like a teenager on a first date.

As we arrived at the restaurant, I was recognised; not by other guests, but of all people, by the proprietor. I felt like some kind of gigolo who used the venue in his conquests of the fairer sex. I have no idea what Jenn thought; my only defence being that she knew I had been there before in another time.

The evening passed as though we were long lost friends. We talked forever. We laughed nervously. In awkward moments we chose to 'people watch' those around us, and we agreed not to mention our dinner date to anyone... although how ever could our liaison remain secret, was a point oblivious to both of us.

When we arrived back at our lodgings, I bid Jenn "Goodnight" with a wave and a smile. She smiled and waved back. My cheeks ached with colour.
The fire in my soul burned as I slept with the events of that evening whirling around my mind; a dream happily fixed on 'repeat'.

The following day revealed a closer bond between Jenn and I; one which others were slowly becoming aware of. Our previous night's escape could not have been more obvious really... there was only one lounge and everyone had been there... except us.

We didn't just travel together to site that morning, we worked together all day, and that evening rode out together to a wine tasting event at a local pottery that subsidised its income with wine and beer sales.
That event started off simple enough. As the flamboyant owner offered up his first gamble, I said little and let others ooze with polite impressiveness. Jenn however, whispered to me that she was not quite so impressed. She, like me it seemed, spoke her mind. I smiled back and gave an affirmative nod that the wine was indeed, awful.
As the evening progressed, the wine didn't get any better. By the time the owner decided to open and pour a red wine without letting it breathe; a matter important to those who understand; I had seen enough. As I gently tore into his presentation, and then proceeded to dismantle the quality, or lack of, of his wine, I found myself playing to an audience of two bored housewives. They wore heavy make-up, their clothes and attendant jewellery perhaps evidence of having married for money not Love; they were evidently out to find someone interesting to be their plaything that night. It seemed I was it. They latched onto my every word.
As the owner tried desperately to win me over with an ever increasing array of 'just in' wines, I played to those housewives,

conscious all the time that out of the corner of my eye, Jenn, having slipped away to browse the wines and pottery on the dusty shelves of the store, was desperately trying to hide her laughter as she reproachfully returned my gaze.

With wines exhausted, I finally prised myself away from the jewel encrusted fingers of those housewives and joined Jenn. I was curious to see what she had found, and perhaps, I simply just wanted to be near her.
As Jenn pointed out a bottle of wine to me, I murmured with approval. It was for us to share one night she informed. She was also clutching a pottery mug, one graced with stars and a moon. On impulse, I took it from her hands, and despite her protests bought it for her. There was only good reason to do so; a thank you to an angel who was fast opening my heart and allowing it to breathe again. I was also completely infatuated; happily trapped by her enchanting spell, and I didn't give a damn. Jenn, as I was to learn, being dedicated to going 'Dutch', paid for the wine.

Another day, another adventure; this time it was to the island lighthouse.
We were, as we always seemed to be now, chaperoned by someone from our group. Were they there to watch over Jenn, protect her from my perhaps evident advances? I didn't know, but I suspected so. And yet, they need not have worried, for Jenn had a confidence about her that I could never hope to aspire to, or take advantage of. She could leave me in the dust of despair at an instant if she so wished. To her, I must have been so obviously besotted, perhaps a fool to be toyed with; one to be let down gently when the game became too serious. I simply had not the slightest clue, and I didn't care.

We climbed the stairs of the lighthouse. Upon reaching the top, Jenn walked one way around the balcony, and I, quite deliberately, went the other way. It seemed the obviously silly thing to do. As we met around the back, our eyes caught each other's, and there was, I swear, something in her gaze I had not seen before.

There was a long pause before we turned our backs on each other and headed back to the stairway.

As we reached them, I stopped to ask the Park Ranger present whether the island ever witnessed the presence of Sea Turtles. I desperately needed a distraction. The ranger replied factually that they did.

There are moments in life when the path you take seems unclear, but you tread it anyway, and there are times when that path appears with neon flashing lights and pointing arrows, but you do not recognise it. I didn't. On declaring I'd never seen a Sea Turtle in the wild, Jenn replied simply:

"We should go looking for sea turtles one day."

That night, while sat next to each other during a trivia quiz with our colleagues, it must have been obvious to everyone, that, if it had not happened already, we were fast becoming an 'item'. We were, after all, exclusively sharing the wine Jenn had brought the night of the tastings - to the exclusion of all others.

Thus, in full view of our colleagues, here was I, as close as I had ever been to a woman I could not shake from my mind. She was simply gorgeous. I didn't have a clue how to deal with my emotions, except perhaps, to allow them to continue along this blind, and I thought, probably stupid, path. The time would surely come when I fell over the precipice of heartbreak I was certain lay somewhere along it.

The following day we headed out for another town and another day of relaxation. Again, I felt Jenn was being protected by a chaperon. Nevertheless, for a fleeting moment, I finally found myself alone with my obsession.

As our eyes met once more, there was, once again, 'that' moment. Was this the time to be brave, to finally risk the slap in the face, the indignation? I felt strangely awkward. I wanted to kiss her but like a teenager, I hesitated. What if we were seen? What would people think of me? But above all, just what would Jenn think of me? How would she react? I so desperately didn't want to spoil the enchanting time I was having in her company. If I kissed her, dared to force myself upon her, it might end here and now; my happily bewitched soul shattered, my heart broken, my embarrassment insurmountable, and worse... my impact on Jenn's own standing, all too great to comprehend, or ever to be forgiven.

I looked away, changed the subject, and moved to leave the place we had found. I didn't know whether to kick myself, grab her and kiss her anyhow, or simply accept that I had reached the boundary of our relationship, the one I believed I would never be allowed to cross over.

I could bear it no longer; another day together but not together was passing by, and another bottle of wine available to share privately, standing ready and waiting. I had to know.

As we drove home from site once more alone together, I finally asked the question I had been terrified to ask. Would Jenn go to the beach with me tonight? You know, to share the bottle of wine, and perhaps just to talk?

I have no idea what else I said. I tried so hard to sound innocuous, but I know those words were filled with apologies and excuses. I got the answer I expected, and perhaps deserved. It was a polite 'not tonight'. A gentle put down. One I was almost relieved to hear. At least this way there was no awkward embarrassment. It could be dealt with as a simple acceptance on my part, graciously received as a thank you for not having me hung, drawn, and quartered in front of everyone. I said no more, and went quietly to my bed that night.

I spent the following day in subservient mood to Jenn. We worked together and thankfully could still laugh together. I had been a fool, but at least I had not been made to look like one. For this I was so very grateful to her.

I hesitated to get into her car that evening for the drive home from site, but Jenn simply told me, in no uncertain terms, to get in. I meekly accepted in the belief that she had taken pity on me

and determined I was harmless.
As we set off, she turned to me, looked into my eyes, and said:

"We can go to the beach tonight..."

Together

It was a simple matter for us to drift away once more from the group that night. As we had done previously, we made our excuses individually to go to our rooms, and then quietly slipped out the door. Thinking back, we must have been so obvious.

The beach, a mere stone's throw away, was all too beckoning. We didn't even bother to head off in another direction, or even walk independently to it. Tonight was now or never, perhaps for both of us, and yet, I was still uncertain of what was to unfold.

The beach was still busy with annoyance when we found a place to settle with our backs to the sand dunes, but it was private enough for talk. I removed the cork from the bottle, poured it into our glasses, and, as we dug our feet into the sand, I offered a simple toast.

We began to talk. Idle chatter at first, I cannot even remember what we discussed; but as the evening passed, and the presence of others thinned, and finally melted away, I began to open my heart. I told Jenn that I found her company enchanting, that she had woken the soul within me to reveal that life was out there. I told her of the dark days of my life these past ten years or more, my time as a local councillor, my research and how it led me to be on Hatteras Island, four thousand miles from home, and now, with the most enchanting woman I'd ever known.

As she listened, so I talked, long into the night.

I finally ran out of story to tell. It was now Jenn's turn.

She told me of her struggles, her past life, her present life, and the crossroads she knew she faced today.

For once in my life, I had learned to listen. I spoke only to question, to comfort, to offer token advice.

As the wine bottle emptied, so the burden of our lives filtered into the sand beneath us.

With the fullest of moons high above, our stories told, and the beach deserted, silence descended. I bowed my head, and turned to look at Jenn, her face beaming in the moonlight, and said simply:

"Your eyes are like Moonbeams, so bright, so full of life. You are the most gorgeous creature I've ever met."

These were not the planned words of a gigolo, nor the saved corny words of Saturday night chat-up lines; they were spontaneous, I meant them in the most intense, sincerest way, and they were words that laid my heart bare.

I did not know what would happen next, perhaps an abrupt end to the night, or maybe a hoped for smile. The response was something I will never forget...

Jenn's face broadened into a dimpled smile. She slowly leaned back against the sand, hair swept to one side, hand cupping the back of her head. She gazed up at the moon and then at me.

I hesitated. Should I kiss her? It was now or never. I moved slowly towards her, glancing nervously into her eyes as I did so. But this was no tease. I moved closer, paused, and then kissed her, gently, but meaningfully. She kissed me back.

If the world had ended, if there had been an audience to that kiss, if the sky had fallen, I would not have known. I would not have cared. I closed my eyes. All my lips could feel all my arms could hold, all my soul could breathe in, felt as though I had been hurled into a dream, a waking dream. One I never wanted to end. If 'magical' is an over-used word, so be it, I can find no other for that moment.

We stayed there, alone on that beach, private in our own world, never straying too far to embarrass, never parting to end.
For all those strange and earthly passions that lie deep within lovers, this was a night where the act of the kiss was the act alone. We needed no more. We were alone in our universe, and content within it.

It was long after I know not when, that we finally decided sleep was something we both needed, for the task that had brought us fatefully together was still to be completed.
We crept to our rooms that night as though two teenagers knowing they had broken the rules. As we said our farewells behind half-closed doors, there was that lingering moment that asked for one more kiss. And yet, as we both knew, one more kiss would not be enough. Our doors closed on the most beautiful night of my life.

The following morning was filled with that awkward low key breakfast where no-one said a word but everyone knew.

In truth, it did not take long into the day before one of our colleagues, someone I had known for years, gazed inquisitively into my eyes. I knew this was time for a confession.

"We need to go for a walk, don't we?" I asked.
A simple nod was her reply.

"I don't know where this is going" I said. "I know that it might just be a holiday romance, but I've never been this happy, or this content."

I confessed I knew my time with Jenn might simply be just a precious few days, or even that the previous night might be all there would ever be, but I was enchanted, bewitched, and entirely happy to be so. Our conversation ended, we returned to work. Nothing further was said.

As I showered and changed for dinner that evening, I saw Jenn through the half-closed door of her bedroom. She was brushing her hair in that purposeful way women with long hair do. I don't know what made me do it but I raced into her room and in sheer devilment, physically lifted her off her feet. She squealed and laughed, told me I was a naughty boy and with the broadest of grins added:

"No-one has ever picked me up like that before."

The delight in my eyes must have told her I wanted to do it again, but as Jenn playfully shooed me out of the door, I turned and gave one last longing look in her direction. Another "shoo" and I obeyed. I knew there would be another time.

Later that night, Jenn stopped by the deliberately open door of my room. As usual I was applying cream to the wheals on my skin. She came in. I grinned and with much tongue in cheek offered to apply cream to her bites if she would apply cream to mine. I expected reproach. What I got was a wonderful, long, perfect leg extended towards me. It was accompanied by a delicate finger which proceeded to point out the bites she had suffered.

Later that night, hoping, that the door to her room would be open, I looked into the corridor. It was. I peered around her bed-room door, almost hesitating to do so for I was still so very conscious of over-stepping the mark with this wonderful, playful, but confident spirit of a woman.
She was reading. She put the book down, and shook her head in the reproach I expected, and yet, there it was again, that huge flashed smile spreading across her face. I closed the door and fell into her arms, only returning to my room when sleep determined once again that I should do so.

The following morning I became the subject of increasing concern for the mosquito bites I had suffered; large wheals, now inflamed, peppered my arms and ankles. But there were more... A band of bites had appeared around my waistline, a place that should have been protected by my T-shirt.

As those bites were being treated by our nurse, so Jenn stepped forward for her treatment. She lifted her T-shirt to reveal identical areas of bites around her waistline... Nobody said a word, the smiles in the room said everything.

Later, as we both sat in the lounge, fidgeting, with only the rain, incessant upon the windows, to distract us from each other, one of our colleagues burst out:

"Will you two go somewhere, there's way too much static around here and I can't concentrate!"

The smiles, the holding hands, and our souls, were now free at last. No matter what we were doing, or where we were going, we could openly be together. Life had become a whole new adventure, for both of us.

For the next four nights we would wait for the others to go to bed before sneaking into one another's room.

What took place those nights will forever remain unknown to you. It is enough to understand that abstinence is possible, even in the most unbridled of moments.

For us, those nights felt like our forever, yet we knew our days together were dwindling, no matter how much we wished they would not.

Apart

The day we knew was coming, but which as all lovers hope will never come, finally arrived… the morning of our departure, the separating of our ways, and of our new found Love.

As each of our colleagues left the shared accommodation to return to their own lives, a benevolent soul granted Jenn and I, exemption from what chores remained. We had been given, what, for all we knew, for all we expected, would be a precious last few hours together.

We went for a drive. We could have driven forever; anywhere. Yet we both knew that however much our hearts yearned for each other, it could not be. Not now, and perhaps not ever.

We stopped some miles distant along the shoreline, I know not where, and made our way to the beach and turned to wander along the shoreline, close but not touching, almost fearful that the act would trigger the tears, tears we knew would fall anyway, but hopefully not just yet, and not in front of one another, for that would be too much to bear.
We walked as far from the crowds as we could, stopped, and faced each other for the inevitable last embrace.

I took Jenn's gentle hands in mine, pressed my forehead to hers, and gazed into her eyes. They were full of a sadness I found difficult to hide in mine. I kissed her. We stood holding each other, swaying ever so gently in comfort, in tune with the roaring swell of the ocean; the sound of the waves ushering our sadness.

The sting of tears crept from the corner of our eyes as we spoke in hope of staying in touch. We talked of her coming to England, of me returning to America; all those things lovers do when partings must happen. We called each other by the pet names that had so spontaneously become ours, as though somehow it would strengthen the bond between us... She was my 'Moonbeam' and to her I was her 'Celt'.

In the silence that followed, it was the ocean, crashing upon the shore that inspired me to whisper:

"The seventh wave is always the biggest."

Jenn squeezed ever more tightly to me as I felt her tremble. I was to learn later that those simple words were to change everything.

There is no greater pain in the world than heartbreak. There is no cure, medically, physically, psychologically, for the feeling of loss. There is no comfort to be found in others, nor their offered words of sympathy. There is only comfort - to be back in the arms of the one you are separated from.

We had to return to our lodgings and make that final break, we both knew it, but there would be one last, symbolic, meal together.

I found it difficult to eat. Conversation was minimal. Silence bathed our broken souls; the impending separation, utterly, unbearable. As we got into the car for the final miles back to our accommodation, tears stained our cheeks.

We arrived in silence, hastily grabbed our bags, and loaded our respective cars in silence. I watched as Jenn waved goodbye one last time before getting into hers.

I climbed into that of our benevolent friend, and waited. I knew

I had to see Jenn leave. It seemed she was taking forever. I looked across the driveway to see her drying the tears from her eyes in the rear view mirror. I watched as she swept her hair aside, checked the mirror once more, and then speed away from my heart... pulling it, and hers, apart in the process.

On the journey to my last night's accommodation before flying home, I kept looking for Jenn, hoping, wishing, to find her car parked on the side of the road.
I have no idea what I would have done if I had seen it... Well, yes I do, I would have jumped rashly from our car, climbed into hers and we would have become two missing children, forever lost to the world, except our own world, somewhere in America. I didn't want to leave her, and I didn't want to lose her, ever.
In some ways it was right that there would be no sign of her, but as we passed the junction I knew she would have taken towards her own home, my heart. I swear, for a moment stopped beating.

That night I retired early, almost indecently early. I wanted to be alone. I was alone. All my thoughts were of the angel who had mesmerised me for two weeks, and who I had just lost.

You do strange things when you are emotionally lost. I chose to examine the beautiful and intricate quilt one of my dear friends had presented to me that week. On the reverse were a series of angels. One had the same name as mine. It was enough. I burst into tears. I repeated Jenn's name over and over again. I cried so hard; hard enough that no sound came from my mouth. My chest hurt. If my heart had burst I would not have cared, nor cried out for help. Only one person could help anyhow, and I didn't even know where, or how, to find her.
I have not the slightest clue when I fell asleep that night, but I do know that I woke to find myself wrapped in that quilt.

The next day, I boarded my flight and sat down at my allotted seat. Without a word I pulled a blanket over me. I didn't wake until I felt the jolt that told me we had landed eight hours later, and four thousand miles from my heart.

I don't remember driving home from the airport that day. What I do remember occurred the following morning as I rose too early as usual to go to work. There was an email in my inbox, and it was from Jenn.
My Moonbeam had written to me.

It was a simple message but one that ended by thanking me for a wonderful time, a time that had made her realise there was more to life than she believed there could be.

I opened my heart in reply.
I tried to remain practical, but I found myself already asking the questions 'What if...' 'Perhaps we could...'
I ended with the simple request that if she would keep writing, then so would I. My heart and soul begged that she would.
She did.

Hope

At first the emails were full of the simple things; as though we were reliving our holiday romance... the happy times, and the sad times; and then the hopes, the dreams, the racing away with the moments began, only to end once more with the utter heartbreak we had endured.

Jenn revealed that she would have stopped for me, and that she too had cried all the way home.

Love had placed two halves of the same heart four thousand miles apart and allowed them to find each other. We just had to work out how to make it whole again.

As the days passed, the flurry of communications intensified.

As I would rise each day to an email from Jenn, so I would reply to make sure she rose to one too, for her day four thousand miles away, started five hours later than mine. As my day ended, so I would come home to her reply, and in return she would come home to mine.

Within a few days we began to use internet messaging and it was not long before those conversations became almost continuous.

Hours and hours of happiness were contained in those messages, for we knew each other's voice, we could hear it in our mind as we read them. It was as though we were only temporarily apart, as though we had been lovers in another life, as though we were slowly, inextricably, being drawn back together again by those messages.

The subjects in those messages were idle, yet purposeful... What was my favourite colour? What was my favourite book? Did I prefer mountains or the beach? Would I wash-up after dinner? There were seventy-seven questions in all. As I threw them back at Jenn, so she dutifully answered them too.

In questions you learn much... and in answers, more. So much of what we responded with, could simply have read 'ditto'. We were twins, perhaps the oddest of twins, but twins nonetheless and we were finding each other again. I felt like a teenager in the first flush of Love, and Jenn was holding my hand as we hurtled down a path I had no idea where it would lead.

As the days passed so we became ever closer, ever more knowing of the other; only the miles, now a fictitious distance, separated us.

And then the day came when we spoke...
It was a simple, short, but magical phone-call. As Jenn answered and as I spoke, each of us broke into laughter only the most intense of emotional releases can muster.
What we spoke of I cannot recall; the tumbled words, the fluttering hearts are all that I remember. It felt as though the distance between us had just gotten so much smaller.
And a few days later our first video chat took place... the intensity of our communications had now become all consuming.
We had been apart just two weeks...

The questions slowly turned serious. Would, could, Jenn come to England? Perhaps just for a week or two, just to see if we were real, if we could live our happiness once more... But Jenn had a career, and she could not abandon her own future, one she had worked so hard to secure. I knew this, but in Love, you do whatever you need to in order to keep it from fading.

And thus, never has a man worked so feverishly to find opportunities for the woman of his infatuation.
I was either lucky, or, I have to concede, Love had a plan... for

many in my circle of contacts worked for a museum or an archaeology company... perfect and fertile ground for enticing a Masters graduate Moonbeam to come and visit.

I laid the offers I had received before Jenn. I felt like a Bowerbird putting on a display to impress the female of his attentions. I sat back and waited, excited, hoping that they would be enough to attract her.

A few days after I had presented my 'gifts' to Jenn, I rose early as usual to find an email in my Inbox.
It had no words, it didn't need any. The image it contained said all it needed to...
Jenn had obtained a Passport...
My heart soared. Jenn was now one step nearer.
Another week passed by. All I could think to ask was when would she be coming over?
The answer came via another email. Again there was no message, just an image...
It was a plane ticket...

From then on, our conversations and emails contained only one subject matter ... "T minus 44 days and counting"... "T minus 43 days and counting"... "T minus 42..."

During those final days apart, our lives became hectic.
Our reunion could have been over in a week or two, but it never entered our heads. It was as though we both expected that reunion would last forever. Jenn had packed her worldly goods into storage. She had said her 'Good-byes'. She had addressed so many things once put off until tomorrow but now being attended to in the heat of the moment.

Thus, as Jenn prepared her life for a new adventure, so I prepared mine too.
I had made the most of my tiny cottage and furnished it as best I could... Two plates, two bowls, two knives, two forks, two cups,

two chairs and a tiny dinner table. A washing machine, a bed, a second hand sofa, a second hand cooker, and a second hand fridge... all the things I thought we would need... All the things I could afford.

The last twenty-four hours before Jenn's plane arrived were a blur. I remember driving to my mother's home, I remember trying to explain all that had happened, and I remember listening to Jenn's sweet voice on the phone... It was slurred... She admitted to me that she had consumed two, large, (very large), bourbons while waiting for her flight. While I found it funny, I could tell that Jenn was a little embarrassed. Thus, the devil in me, being so full of exuberance, passed the phone to my mother... much to Jenn's horror.

I listened as Jenn tried to explain to her, in the best of slightly drunk concentration, that she was not normally like this... that she didn't get drunk, that she could act appropriately; that she would not embarrass her son...

It was the first time they had ever spoken to each other.

I finally took the phone from my mother's hand, wished Jenn a good flight, ended the call, and turned to face my mother.

"She sounds lovely." she said...

As I lay down to sleep that night, the time for Jenn and I, would begin in little more than eight hours time...

Reunion

There are no words to describe the intensity of those last few hours apart.

I slept fitfully that night but was awake more than early enough to find myself wondering if I should drive to the airport in the full knowledge that I would arrive there more than an hour before Jenn's flight was due to land. I wondered no more and headed out.

The drive was on empty roads, yet I found myself walking into the arrivals lounge barely twenty minutes before her flight arrived; it was early. I grabbed the biggest bunch of flowers I could find, and positioned myself as near I dared to the Customs Hall doors and waited. I could not have been more obvious; and I was wearing tie-dye.

Perhaps ninety eternal minutes must have passed. There was no sign of Jenn's smile.

I became aware that I was the subject of conversation among a small group of female 'Olympic Ambassadors'; this being the time of the London Olympics; who were standing nearby. They had noted my constant fretful pacing, all the while flowers carefully held aloft.

I could stand it no more. As red faced as I could be, I asked one of them if they could find out whether a beautiful woman wearing tie-dye was perhaps waiting on her luggage in the customs area, or worse, had been held by Immigration officials... for that small voice of fear becomes so irrationally loud when Love is so tantalisingly close yet so far out of reach.

A few moments later, the woman returned. She smiled. I guessed, I hoped, she had seen my Jenn in the luggage hall... I readied myself for the embrace that I knew would be overwhelmed with emotion. We had been apart for so long.... all seventy seven days of it.

A few minutes later, she who I had longed for, adored from afar, and who had been torn so painfully from my arms, burst through the arrival hall doors... and she was toting the largest of excess luggage I've ever seen. It was an observation that the significance of which did not dawn on me at the time, but one that I now realise meant, quite simply, that while I was still unsure I could be the man she wanted, Jenn had pretty much already made up her mind. I, in that moment of blind revelation, had only one thing in focus... the smile on her face; my Moonbeam was just a few feet from my arms.

We kissed long. We hugged tight. We gazed infatuated at each other. There was only us... and we were oblivious to the chaos we had caused among her fellow travellers, each trying to squeeze past her copious luggage now strewn across the exit from the Customs Hall.

We paused to smile at the Ambassadors, each with hands clasped and head adoringly set at an angle as they gazed upon our lovers embrace.

It was Jenn who brought us both back to Earth. We needed to get out of the airport, for there was still that nagging, inane doubt that we might be torn apart again by the appearance of Immigration Officials wanting another 'chat'.

At this point, I have to make a confession... I had forgotten where I had parked the car. I dared not tell Jenn, although it was to become apparent the moment we were confronted by the entrances to three separate car parks, all nestled close enough to one another to be connected, and yet separated by a chasm that could only be negotiated by going back down to the ground floor and crossing over to the next one... and the Lifts were out of order... in all of them.

Undeterred, I strode confidently to the first car park and headed up the stairs, valiantly, and I hoped, manfully, hauling Jenn's heaviest suitcase behind me.

Was the car on the second storey; nope; perhaps the third? Nope, not that one either.

The Love of my life soon realised what was up. I felt an idiot. This was not a good start. Back down two flights of stairs we went and crossed over to the adjacent car park to repeat the same exercise. Jenn, in a loving attempt to help jog my memory, asked questions...

"What car did I have?"
"Skoda" I replied.
"We don't have those in America. What does it look like?" she said.

I replied that it was a Saloon, and looked a bit like a Volkswagen. This was not much help either for the only Volkswagen Jenn could recall was a Beetle. I didn't have a Beetle.

"What colour is it" she asked helpfully.

Being colour-blind I had to think about this carefully.
Fortunately, I'm one of those people who remembers useless bits of information, thankfully this was the moment my memory chose to reveal one of those 'bits'. According to the manual in the glove box of the car, my Skoda was 'teal' coloured.

"Teal" I replied confidently.

This, as it turned out, was not a lot of help. The car park was dimly lit; the only visible colours were 'light' and 'dark'.

As we reached the third storey of the second car park, I suddenly spotted a familiar looking estate car. Something inside me believed my car was parked behind it.
It was.
I was grateful for the darkness in that car park; for my face was bright red and sinking rapidly between my shoulders. I feared that Jenn would create a scene, 'lose it', or shed a tear in a tantrum because I had made us look perhaps not a little stupid. But no, all Jenn could do was laugh; the relief on my face would have been all far too evident if she could but have seen it.

The moment we drove under the car park exit barrier felt like it represented all that could have stood in our path to be together. Out there was the world and we were free to explore it.
I squeezed Jenn's hand, kissed it and looked briefly into her eyes. Here she was, by my side once more.
I picked up my phone and rang my mother and said, simply:

"Mum, I've got my Jenn."

It was all she needed to hear.

We drove in silence for most of the way to our first destination, just occasionally touching each other's hand in reassurance. The feeling was surreal. We really were sitting next to each other.

Jenn had said that there were three things she wanted to do on her first day in England.
The first required a small market town deep in the Sussex weald, one that defined all that is quintessentially England, and the town of Midhurst fits that bill perfectly.
It was there that I had planned to have our first breakfast together... It was to be enjoyed by the side of the town's ubiquitous 'village' duck pond.

We selected a small bench by it, sat down, and tucked into the fresh bread, brie and grapes, that I had prepared... exactly as Jenn had requested.

I felt pleased with myself.

As we ate, all I could do was turn and smile at Jenn. She smiled back. Occasionally our hands would touch. We were really there, together. Even as it began to drizzle with rain, we remained unmoved. This was our moment, one of peace, one of wonder, and one of pure content.

The raindrops had other plans though, as they escalated rapidly into a downpour, we came back to reality, raced to the car and drove off, heater running full blast as we quietly steamed. We were soaked through but unperturbed. The moment, however short, had been perfect.

As Jenn dozed fitfully, for she had had a long flight and, as I was to learn later, had endured it with little or no sleep; I drove on through the English countryside.

Jenn's second request involved Stonehenge, arguably one of the most iconic landmarks in England, if not the world, and a significant 'fix' for Jenn's archaeological passion...

We bided our time in the long queue at the entrance, eventually to pause only briefly in the museum before heading out to add our own footsteps to the millions who have trodden the monument's circular path before us.

A photo taken, we reached the most distant part of the circuit just as the rain began to fall yet again. Still soaking from the first downpour, we cared not and slowly made our way back to my now evidently 'teal' coloured car that wasn't a Volkswagen Beetle.

As Jenn dozed off once more, I contemplated that in the first hours of our life together I had lost the car and drowned my sweet Jenn, twice. And yet, her response had been one only of laughter. I have never been so hapless, and yet never so happy.

The last three hours of the long drive to our new home together were completed in silence, the beautiful woman by my side, sleeping peacefully as I ploughed my way through the English countryside.

Jenn woke just as I turned into the long drive to our tiny home, a small cottage set among an orchard, deep in the rural heart of Devon, and a long way from anywhere. It could not have been more private, or more perfect for two lovers to discover if they were meant to be.
I unloaded Jenn's luggage while she toured our tiny abode. It met with her approval.
With the basics unpacked, we headed for the local Inn.
With Jenn's third request; English fish and chips suitably washed down by a traditional Irish stout, we headed back to our cottage. It had been a long, emotional day, but our adventure had well and truly begun.

There was something of a nervous trepidation as we faced our first night together.
We had finally been unshackled by the Love we had yearned for. We were only us, a couple who had fallen heavily for each other in unexpected circumstances, a couple who had endured a separation neither wanted. And yet, now, when we were finally free of all restraint, there was to be that awkward moment when we would climb into the only bed we had.
And yet, in the dark silence of our surroundings that night, the mere presence of each to the other was all we needed.
We fell rapidly into a deep sleep, little spoon, big spoon, secure in the knowledge that the Celt and the Moonbeam were together again.

Learning

The following morning, I woke early. With Jenn still asleep, I crept out of the bedroom, shaved, and headed for the kitchen. I made that beautiful woman a simple breakfast of coffee, and an omelette. I knew this was her perfect breakfast for it was the answer to Question twenty-three…

As I brought it into the bedroom, Jenn was trying desperately to sham sleep, that huge beaming smile of hers, a complete giveaway.

"Thank you punkin." was all she needed to say.

My heart glowed.

Some time later that I was to find out Jenn had heard me in the kitchen and figured out what I was doing. Her response had been to post just four words on social media:

"My god, he cooks!"

We truly were on a voyage of discovery.

There was much to do during our first day together.

Jenn unpacked her luggage while I cleaned and pottered around, vaguely tidying up in that way that only a man can. Each time we passed each other in the hallway, in the doorways, in the rooms; there was always a kiss, or the simple reassuring brush of hands.

We knew that to stop for too long would end all hope of setting up our little home that day.

At some point we headed out to do some vital shopping for food... this was important because the only sustenance in the house had just been consumed for Breakfast...

Watching Jenn experience an English supermarket for the first time was fascinating.
As she reached for the organic fruit and vegetables, so I reached for the ordinary stuff. This caused some concern on her part.

"I like to know what I'm putting in my mouth" she advised.

I didn't twig the significance of her comment until we stopped to buy some chicken pieces. As she turned over the pack to read the label, I just added a pack to the shopping basket.

"It's chicken," I said, puzzled by the apparent need she had to study everything we were buying.
She replied that she was checking for water and salt content.

"The label doesn't tell me anything" She lamented.

I tried in vain to answer her questions...
Were the chickens truly 'free range' or simply penned up by the tens of thousands in dark, acrid, barns? What did they eat? How did they process them? Was it humane? These things, as I was to learn of Jenn, were extremely important. I was also to learn that my tie-dye wearing infatuation was somewhat more of an 'eco-Nazi' than even I was. If it were possible, I loved her even more for that.
As we moved around the store, staple foods, wine (ahem), and the occasional treat, were pre-requisites; while items for meal-planning would be studied intently before being discarded or ending up in the basket.

LOOKING FOR SEA TURTLES

At some point Jenn spotted a carefully packaged pair of Sweet Potatoes and burst into spontaneous laughter...
She beckoned me over and pointed to the label.
According to its declaration, they had come from the 'Sunshine state of North Carolina, USA' - Jenn's home.
She'd already photographed them for her social media blogs by the time she explained to me that sweet potatoes in North Carolina were so ubiquitous that they were commonly found in giant mounds by the roadside. It would be Jenn's turn to cook that night... for I had not the foggiest idea how to deal with the somewhat earthy, rustic looking 'Sunshine state' food that had just gone into the basket.

Back home and it was time for that first evening meal together.
I duly laid our tiny table for two with knives, forks and spoons, and two glasses. I then the wine bottle, filled the glasses, and duly lit the candle in the (slightly chipped) single candlestick I had brought, romantically I thought, for our mealtimes. Although it was never said, the lighting of that candle was to become very symbolic, for both of us.

My proud sweep of the hand to denote my best efforts at providing a 'Silver Service' array of cutlery that night was met with a little surprise.
As we sat down to dinner I watched Jenn promptly abandon the knife and spoon and proceed to use just the fork to devour the entire meal. I had no idea that all the required mashing, cutting, and consuming of a modest three course meal could be achieved with just one item of cutlery.
I watched, fascinated, barely able to take my eyes off the performance. I of course, maintained my very British way of using a knife, fork, and spoon... much to Jenn's equal amusement.

After we had cleared the table, I did the washing up. Jenn apparently hated that part but offered moral support by hopping up onto the worktop adjacent to the sink, and watching me; her

33

mere presence, enough to switch on that manly light inside me and encourage something of a performance of my own. Hell, if she had asked me to go out and kill something for dinner with my bare hands, I would have done it... not that animal lover Jenn would have ever let me... she would, as I was to learn, open a window to set free the tiniest of flies, even if it was mid-winter...

The days passed quickly during that first week. It was a time of discovery, of self, of each other, and for Jenn, of the land that was to be her new home.
Among those discoveries though, it was perhaps the personal habits that were the most endearing for both of us.

One of the first that had to be overcome, for me at least, was the rather bad manners of my intestines... yes, the occasional, and often loud retort was something I have never mastered complete control of.
When the moment finally came and I could not hold it in any longer one night, it was already too late to make it from the table to a safe distance without causing some concern on the part of Jenn that I was about to throw up her lovingly prepared meal... so I let go.
There was an awkward silence. Jenn's glass of wine paused midway to her mouth. I wanted to hide, to offer my profuse apologies, to confess to my near guaranteed relationship breaking habit.
Jenn slowly put down her glass, and grabbed the table with both hands. I had no idea what was about to. I was becoming alarmed. My heart began to race. This was it, our first argument...
Her next move was simple and potently effective. She gulped, and let rip with a window vibrating, scorched earth, belch.
My mouth fell open.
Another silence followed.

"Phew, I'm glad we've got that out of the way" I sighed.

It was enough. Within days we were bathing together... an interesting exercise in itself... how two six foot tall people can bathe in a four foot something bath. The overhead shower though proved to be considerably easier.

Odd though these arrangements may seem to some, for us it felt entirely natural, uninhibited, and a little wondrous at that.

As each new day in our lives together dawned, so we would plan an adventure and head off somewhere. I wanted to show Jenn every square mile of her new home; her mere presence breathing a life into my soul I had never felt before. It was more than enough to spur me ever onward in my endeavours.

One place that quickly became our favourite haunt was Hartland Quay. Amounting to no more than a small hotel and disused quay, its setting, nestled among a tortured coastline of jagged rocks and crashing waves, faced due west. Thus, from here we could watch the sun set towards Jenn's homeland before enjoying a pint of beer in the hotel.

It was also a convenient place to leave the car and explore the nearby footpaths.

I led Jenn south from there one day to see a nearby waterfall that plunged spectacularly onto the beach. What caught her eye was not the waterfall though but a rather insignificant peak, just a few hundred yards south of the hotel we had started from.

It rose steeply from a tiny trough of land and tapered into a small point before plunging 200 feet into the Atlantic Ocean.

I dutifully followed as she headed across the field that led to it. As we approached, I realised it was a hell of a lot more steep than I thought; I could only win the race to the top if I cheated and dragged Jenn back... which of course I did...

Once at the top, we were both surprised to find that the summit hid a tiny plateau, just large enough for two people to sit, and, as Jenn established, just large enough to include room for a small tablecloth.

The stunning beauty of the location, coupled with the guaranteed privacy it afforded, ensured Jenn and I were to picnic there frequently; she, taking great care to ensure that not the tiniest scrap of waste would be left behind or be snatched from our hands by the ever present sea breeze to soil our pristine 'happy place'.

I had now learned there was a little bit of 'Earth Mother' in Jenn too.

There was a serious side to learning though, and that focused on Jenn's ability to drive.... on the left, as opposed to her native homeland's right side of the road.

At first it was a simple case of whether Jenn could familiarise herself with a manual transmission. My car didn't make that easy, for it had six gears.

What I'd also overlooked was that Jenn would have to change gear using her left instead of right hand.

This was not to prove as hard as I thought, although, for some strange reason, 'third' was to become the least used gear in her repertoire. For the unknowing, 'third' was sandwiched between 'first' and 'fifth'; thus, going from second into an accidental fifth with Jenn driving was a sort of juddery affair, while changing down from fourth into first instead of third proved downright terrifying...

Jenn could get going quick enough though. Even roundabouts proved to be simple... in fact she managed to master those to a level where the avoiding motorist would be forced to hit his horn in disgust at her manoeuvre; to which she would reply by waving gaily in the rear view mirror before zooming off into the distance...

It was not long before Jenn also learned the various profanities that we Brits excel at when driving too. She had already heard most of them from me as I directed them towards other motorists on the road; indeed she had chastised me often enough for their use... Until that was, the day came when, while Jenn was driving, a car attempted to pull out into our path without looking.

Jenn braked hard and swerved neatly to avoid him. As she did so, she shouted "asshole" (as only Americans can), in his general direction. I was impressed, but realising that the windows were wound down and that he must therefore have heard what she said, it was all I could do to slump as low in the seat as possible for fear of being associated with this aggressive woman driver I had no knowledge of. Seeing my embarrassment, Jenn went on to justify her outburst... which of course made things worse... because all I could do was laugh. The more she tried to dig herself out of the hole she had put herself in, the more I laughed, and the more I would remind her of the way she chastised me for the same reason. I finally stopped laughing when the slaps became painful...

I learned too that Jenn was very capable with what might traditionally be termed 'man's work'...

That inbred, slightly macho thing all men have, and to which I aspired, set me to work cutting the grass in the little orchard surrounding our cottage one day; my weapon of choice, a rather battered but trusty little petrol mower that had spent most of its life chewing up the meadow grass at my previous home. Today though, it finally chose to show its age.
As I got half way around the garden, the lever that set the height of the cut, broke. As the mower spontaneously slumped to the ground, so the motor cut out with a sudden 'whump'.

For several minutes I attempted to tie the lever back up to the required notch, but trying to hold up the heavy engine with one hand while tying a wire knot with the other proved impossible.
Jenn, now curious as to why I had only cut half the grass, came out to see what was going on. I proceeded to explain the reason in that way one does when trying to describe complex technical processes to someone you perceive could not possible understand.
As Jenn, ever loving, offered to help, I declared that it was a messy

job and I didn't want her getting into the oily sweaty state I was already in... you know.... that man thing again... but Jenn was having none of it.

Having figured out what my problem was, she brushed me aside, and with both hands promptly hoisted up the engine housing and directed me to tie the lever off where I needed it. I wasted no time, terrified that she would drop the weighty engine and possibly hurt herself.

A few moments later, I beckoned her to let go.

I fired up the mower, looked down at it puttering contentedly once more, and then glanced up at Jenn with awe. She flicked her long hair over her shoulders, simply said:

"Redneck's Daughter" and walked back into the house...

She emerged several minutes later with a mug of hot tea. I gazed into her eyes as she handed it to me.

She could do no wrong.

A few days later, our little cottage was finally connected to the Internet and thereby the outside world. Jenn now had unlimited access to communicate with her myriad family and friends, all keenly awaiting reports from this side of the Atlantic Ocean.

As the installer left, Jenn eagerly set to work connecting the router and all her other IT equipment to our electricity supply. She had several adaptors, each necessary to convert our 220 volts to the American 110 volts she needed for the various devices she had brought with her. I left her to it while I prepared dinner.

I had not been in the kitchen for more than a few minutes when there was an almighty blue flash and a loud 'pop'. Everything in the kitchen went dead.

In an instant I realised that Jenn must have blown the electrics in the house, and a millisecond later, on failing to hear any sound from her, panicked that she had electrocuted herself.

I flew out of the kitchen door to see Jenn wide eyed and rooted to the spot. On the floor in front of her, a Christmas tree of assorted plugs and voltage transformers, all artfully connected to a single multi-socket extension lead, lay smouldering insidiously; the blackened socket on the wall to which it was all connected providing the evidence of a chronically overloaded circuit.

She looked at me like some naughty child caught red-handed and expecting a scolding. It was never going to happen. As she blurted out her excuses, I just put my finger to her lips, asked if she was OK, and then knelt down to disassemble the still hot Christmas tree. This time, my technical explanation about what she needed to do would make no concession for possible ignorance, it didn't need to; Jenn understood every word.

Our little cottage was finally looking like the Love nest we wanted it to be.

We didn't have much in the way of basic needs; a television for example, was never even contemplated; Jenn and I had no need of it; we could, as we often did, simply sit there, quietly dabbling on the Internet, reading, or lying curled up together in the comfort and peace only lovers find. Sometimes, messages would pass between us electronically so as not to disturb that peace, and sometimes a look was enough for one to know what the other was thinking. Words were rarely required and even fewer used.

We were finally a couple, 'significant others', lovers, undisturbed by the world outside, and content in the one we had created for ourselves.

Work

I t was not long before I had to return to work.
It was a forty minute drive to my employer's office, which, with long hours spent there, meant I would have to leave Jenn at seven in the morning and know that she would not see me until around six that evening. Each work-day was therefore like a terrible parting again, but one tempered with the certain knowledge that we would see each other less than twelve hours later... not weeks later, just hours later.

Yet, as I arrived home each night, there, stood waiting in the hallway to greet me, or sometimes rather coquettishly, simply calling my name from the lounge or kitchen would be this gorgeous woman I had not seen or held all day. It was time for long lost lovers to greet each other once more.
What went on during some of those greetings I dare not say, but suffice to say that the voice of Jenn's mother on video-chat frequently advising us to "Get a room!" is perhaps enough for you to know...

The day finally came though when Jenn could re-launch her own career.
I don't remember exactly when we got her started as a volunteer at the local museum, or working on cataloguing finds for a local archaeology company, but I know she settled in almost immediately, and was soon a regular at both, relabelling entire unsorted archives of ceramics, creating sets for educational purposes, and

all the while routinely challenging expert opinions on some of the assorted finds... She was truly in her element.

The fact that these finds, all English, were being sorted and identified by an American, should perhaps demonstrate Jenn's amazing knowledge on the subject; little wonder that she had already been professionally published on several occasions by the time we had fallen for each other. I was therefore not a little proud of the rising star that had chosen to be part of my life.

Her prowess, and the compliments she received, also made me quickly realise that I had to do everything I could to support her future, even at the expense of my own employment.

With only one car though, and my needing it for business travel, her journey to work had to be determined by the local bus service. Fortunately, it passed close to my workplace.

Thus, every morning, we would drive to the bus stop, and wait in our car for it to arrive.

Just as it would heave into view, Jenn would kiss me good-bye and race to catch it. I would then drive to work, and, a short while later, receive a text to say she had arrived safe. This was always a relief to me... despite us both being mature adults...

At the end of Jenn's workday, she would return to the bus stop where I had left her that morning, and walk down to my workplace, usually arriving shortly before I too finished for the day.

I never tired of seeing her sat there in our Reception area each day. It was as though a public affirmation that we were an item. The glow in our cheeks said everything.

The drive home those evenings was always conducted with hands firmly on each other's leg, almost as a re-bonding and re-assurance that we were back together, even though we had never really been apart.

At times that feeling was surreal, but mostly it was just wondrous.

Protocol

J enn made it clear that she did not 'do' dresses. Her mum, in fact, assured me that it had happened only once before, forcibly, for her Prom night. My problem was... I had been invited to be the guest speaker at a 'Black-Tie' affair... a dress for Jenn was therefore mandatory.

I broke the news to her as gently as I could. Her face fell. This was not going to be easy.

My gambit was to suggest a day out in the City of Exeter, and, if she should perhaps see something she liked while we were there, maybe she would at least try it on.

Since Jenn was tall, slim and high-waisted, I already had a particular store in mind. Thus, when we arrived in Exeter, I made a beeline straight for it, towing Jenn along like a reluctant child behind me.

As we approached the store, Jenn could see the price tags on some of the dresses in the shop window. She halted, dug her heels in and remained rooted to the spot, declaring:

"Nope, looks expensive, not going in there." And that was that.

Despite my willingness to spend whatever it was going to take to find something she would be prepared to wear, Jenn promptly turned a sharp ninety degrees, and headed off purposefully away from the store... pulling me along with her. I didn't have any choice... when we were out in the big wide world; our hands spent virtually all their time firmly locked together, as if in fear of los-ing one another again.

We spent the next couple of hours touring every fashionable (and unfashionable) shop we could find, hunting for something that would be to her liking. I didn't mind doing this for it was not as though Jenn would spend hours searching through rack after rack of dresses. She would merely approach a store, take one look in the window and determine that it was either too expensive, too chic, both, too dull, or worth closer inspection. The latter cat-egory proved to be elusive, very elusive... we didn't stop long enough anywhere for her to try something on.

As Jenn systematically vetoed each store, so I found myself sounding like some 'pull-the-string to hear me talk' toy as I repeated my original plan. Nevertheless, it was fascinating to watch a woman, with a born dislike of dressing up, search for something she really didn't want to wear...

Eventually, I called a halt, found a small café, and beckoned Jenn to sit down and eat something while we figured out our next move.

As we munched our way through a traditional English afternoon tea, Jenn's mood brightened. She had studied the contents of all the various shaped and sized pots that constitute English High Tea, but hadn't entirely figured out what they were all for... so I asked her to pour. I could have been sat at the Mad Hatter's tea party...

As we finished, I took her hand and gently pleaded with her to return to the store I had first tried to get her to venture into. My somewhat faked re-assurance that it was not as expensive as it looked, was helped dramatically by the practical realisation that time was running out. Soon all the stores would start to close. That, and the fact that we had already visited every other clothes shop in town to no avail, finally did the trick.

As we approached the store, Jenn, still dragging back a little, spotted the sales rack just inside the entrance; and there, right at the front of the rack, fully visible from the street, was the perfect high-waisted evening dress. It was also the perfect size, and had the perfect '75% reduced' price tag attached to it.

It was all the encouragement she needed.

Jenn made a beeline for the dress, snatched it off the rail, and headed to the changing room for a fitting. I followed, but with a firm "no Punkin", was instructed to wait in the shop. For all her as-suredness in life, dressing up, it seemed, was something Jenn was decidedly uncomfortable about. I had a feeling there was more to it than that.

Minutes later, she re-emerged... not in the gown I was about to buy, but already back in her jeans and t-shirt. The dress was care-fully draped over her arm, and her face was beaming with satis-faction.

For something less than a quarter of what it might have cost me, Jenn had finally picked her dress, but I was not permitted to see her in it before the moment we set off for the event.

That night I was ready far too early as usual, so wandered into the lounge to wait for Jenn. I figured it would be some while before she emerged from the bedroom.

'Some' while became a 'long' while...

I started to think about the drive to the venue and figured we needed to be leaving soon. My mind then, began to focus on what could be taking Jenn so long.

Now, I know it is something of a tradition for many women to keep their man waiting, but I knew Jenn never wore make-up, (she never needed it), nor did it ever take her long to get ready to go anywhere, ever.

Thus, figuring that she might be having second thoughts, or per-haps was struggling with her dress, I committed that cardinal sin of men and headed for the bedroom to see what the delay was.

I didn't get that far.

There, in the hallway, in her chosen full length, blue, evening dress, busily brushing her long golden hair was somebody I'd never seen before. She was tall; her figure, perfect; her looks flawless. She was a debutant who had clearly got lost on her way to the Ball. I coughed politely. The vision spun round.

It was that moment in the film 'Calamity Jane' when Doris Day is seen in a dress for the first time. Unlike Calamity though, Jenn, with little or no self-awareness, was still concerned about her hair. She turned back to the mirror and began to brush it once more.

As I approached her, she started. I think she was a little concerned that I might be angry at the time she was taking. Nothing could have been further from the truth. As I gazed into her slightly nervous eyes, I slowly and very gently, took the hairbrush from her hand while clasping the other, and whispered:

"You're the most gorgeous creature I've ever seen. Come on beautiful. Let's go."

As we walked down the driveway to the car, I could not have been more proud, nor strutted so obviously like a peacock as I linked arms with her. I confess, it also concerned me a little as to whether Jenn would complete the Calamity Jane moment by tripping over her dress and falling into a puddle. Our audience of Owls and a few bats though had other things on their minds. Nevertheless, I was so mesmerised by the vision on my arm that it was I who almost tripped over - in my haste to run around the car and open the door for her. Making very sure her dress was not trapped in it, I closed the passenger door, raced around to the driver's side, jumped in, prayed the car would start (it did), and hurtled off down the lane.

When we arrived at the reception area for the event, Jenn was holding my arm about as tightly as I think she could. For all her carefree demeanour, Jenn was terrified.

When the moment of our announcement came, Jenn took a deep breath and with one arm still looped around mine, the other flustering with her dress, we entered the room.

It might have been about five minutes, but I think a lot less, before she was surrounded by most of the men present. Somewhere at the back of that crowd I was still waiting for my personal welcome and first drink...

The speech went well; they gave me a commemorative piece of glassware to prove it. As for Jenn, she was a natural debutant... although it is perhaps the memory of watching her teach the chairman how, from the full silver service of cutlery available; to eat the entire three course meal by just using the table fork, that will stay with me forever...

Animals

There were spells when Jenn would not have enough work to occupy her, but her boredom never lasted long.

One of her first pre-occupations had been to start feeding and observing the "critters" as she called them that visited our Bird Table and garden.
Faced with a whole catalogue of birds and animals not found in her own country, it became my task to identify them for her. Thus, I would often arrive at work to find an image from Jenn asking me to put a name to what was currently pecking hell out of our bird feeder.

Given that we lived in such a rural location, it was not surprising that over the next few weeks I was to reel off most of the British garden bird catalogue. Occasionally, my response would come with an added 'Wow' as something I had rarely, or even never seen before, put in an appearance.

There was one day however, when things got just a little more surreal.

As usual, I was at work, and, as usual, Jenn sent me an image with the now familiar enquiry of 'What's this bird?'
The picture revealed a short, dumpy, well-rounded, and rather timid bird I identified as a wild French Partridge... The backdrop however, was not of our garden, but one of our kitchen floor... In

the middle of which, said Partridge was contentedly pecking at a small pile of grain Jenn had thoughtfully placed there for it.

This, I have to tell you, is not an everyday occurrence... Partridges in England are game birds, and usually shot at for sport. Thus, they have an inbuilt fear of humans far beyond that of their feathered kin.

Puzzled and somewhat surprised, I asked the seemingly obvious question:

"What's a Partridge doing in our kitchen?"

Jenn replied as though the appearance of such a bird in the kitchen was routine...

"Oh, I just called him and he came running up to the kitchen for some food."
"His name's Theodore." she added...

A few days later I was to witness this extraordinary meeting first-hand.

We were sitting in the lounge when Jenn jumped up and exclaimed:

"Theodore!"

I watched in disbelief as 'Theodore' came running up to the kitchen door.

Jenn opened it, and, as I stood back, 'Theodore' duly hopped up the three steps that led to the door from the garden, fluttered over the threshold and trotted into the kitchen to take food from Jenn's hand.

Sated, he simply turned his back, trotted back out the door, hopped down the three steps, and wandered off into the undergrowth from whence he came.

Jenn looked at me with childlike glee. All I could do was stare back open-mouthed.

It was not just for this moment that I was to add 'Snow White' to my list of affectionate terms for Jenn. There was to become a catalogue of unusual wildlife encounters over the coming weeks. The day I came face to face, literally, with a wild red fox was one of them...

That particular morning I got up to go to work as normal, kissed a sleep feigning Jenn on the forehead, whispered "I Love you" and headed for my morning ablutions and hurried breakfast.

As I opened the front door to leave, there, in front of me, was our week's trash bag, shredded, its contents littered for several feet in every direction.

My immediate reaction was to cuss the local farm dogs that appeared to live free range in the area, but I was wrong. As I began to pick up the pieces, out of the corner of my eye I spied the face of guilt peering around the corner of our tiny home. It was a wild red fox. He was little more than ten feet away.

After a short staring match, and with the fox showing no intention of running off; I slow-motioned my way back inside the house to wake Jenn. She was already sat up in bed, clearly aware that something was up.

I motioned a finger to my lips and whispered:

"There's a fox outside!"

Jenn merely pointed to the window and said:

"Yes, I can see him."

I spun round to come eye to eye with the same damn fox who was now staring at us both through the bedroom window not two feet the other side of the glass...

He too was suitably named and photographed repeatedly by Jenn over the next few weeks.

When I think about it, it amazed me that this fox never once appeared to take any notice of Maise and Mercedes, our Bantam Wyandotte hens, busily scratching around in their pen... even in broad daylight. In truth, they didn't appear to take much notice of him either. Snow White had evidently given them all a good talking to about being nice to each other...
As for "Theodore" I soon discovered he had friends... three Pheasants to be precise. Naturally, I had to ask Jenn their names.

"Sylvester" She replied.

When asked to identify which one of the identical birds was Sylvester, she replied:

"all three of them"... I should have known.

As the weeks passed, we continued our tours of the local beauty spots, only this time, with a much greater focus on wildlife. It was hard not to; it kept getting in the way of the car.
I could merely pull off the road somewhere, and invariably something suitable impressive, photogenic, or rarely seen, would appear on cue...
A sixteen point antlered Red Deer Stag appeared about five minutes after I had described them to Jenn. The local Exmoor ponies, readily spotted by even the most basic wildlife enthusiast, appeared with a couple of new-born foals for added measure; 'twins' for Jenn to squeal at.
Things got a little ridiculous when, on one such grand tour across the moors, Jenn mentioned she wanted to see what, from her description, I deduced were Highland cattle. I laughed and perhaps in a rather humouring way explained they didn't roam around Exmoor but in the north of Scotland, several hundred miles away...

Well, apparently not.

Twenty minutes later, as I rounded a corner, there, in front of me and blocking the road, was a small herd of said beasts, complete with now mandatory baby calf.

Even in the depths of a dark English winter wildlife was still to be seen or heard when Jenn was around.

As we arrived home to our cottage from the ubiquitous pint down the local Inn one night, we heard an owl hooting. It was a male Tawny Owl with his classic 'Tu-Whit' call. Jenn had never heard a Tawny Owl before. Thus when another owl signalled 'Tu-Whoo' I had to explain to Jenn that these two were in fact a male and female pair and not two separate species. This completely freaked her out.

She adored her "Owlies" as she was to call them, but I'm not so sure they adored her, especially when she started to mimic their calls....

Within days, it wasn't just one pair of Owls that welcomed us home, but several...

With the bill for bird seed now amounting to several pounds of the stuff every week, I'm rather glad Jenn didn't take to feeding those owls... or for that matter, the fox.

Beliefs

I t was not long before I started to venture even further in my introduction of England to Jenn. She had fallen in Love with the wild moorlands of Devon, and in particular, Dartmoor. So I took her to a particularly remote and beautiful part of it. Somewhere that had a secret.

We parked by a moorland reservoir and proceeded to walk around it. As we reached the furthermost point, I turned away from it and led Jenn up a rather eerie track, hemmed, as it was, on both sides by a dark, and moss laden forest of pine trees.

"There be Trolls" she advised.

I could relate to this, for I wanted to show her something almost as mythical; a Neolithic Stone Circle.

These things litter large parts of England, some better preserved than others. Fernworthy's Stone Circle was not only well preserved, but one surrounded by ancient burial mounds. It also had a 'processional' stone lined avenue leading up to it, the enveloping trees doing everything they could to enhance the risk of Trolls attending whatever event unfolded there...

In complete silence we crept, almost reverentially up to the Stone Circle and, hand in hand, walked into the centre of it.
It was a deeply spiritual moment. I do not know why, but it

was. Perhaps there was more to the 'trolls' expectation than I thought...

With a continued feeling of something ever watching of our presence, I turned to face Jenn. I took her hands in mine, pressed my forehead to hers, and closed my eyes. I whispered:

"I Love you. I don't ever want to lose you."

My words felt as though they had been absorbed by the ground beneath us, as a gentle rustle, I hoped of approval, caressed the surrounding trees. I opened my eyes to see a tear rolling down Jenn's cheek. We kissed.

We must have lingered there for several minutes, only finally breaking apart when voices could be heard coming up the nearby track. As those voices yomped past the Stone Circle and on towards the open moorland, a few turned their heads towards us. What they must have thought of two people, dressed in tie-dye, and stood hand-in-hand in the middle of a Stone Circle, I have no idea. 'Damn Hippies' it might have been.

Spiritual places, especially those connected to ancient beliefs, and in particular, Celtic beliefs, were to become a magnet for Jenn and I. And so it was not long before I took her to Glastonbury... one does not fall in Love with a hippie and not take them to Glastonbury, a town as 'out there' as 'out there' can get.

For the unknowing, Glastonbury is pretty much the centre of the universe if your lifestyle is slightly left (or right) of centre. This suited us just fine.

I had no idea what Jenn would make of the place as I parked the car by the ancient abbey but after a short tour of the ruins and it's museum, I led Jenn into the town centre.

Within minutes, Jenn had ventured into the first store offering all things incense and crystal related.

A pattern was soon to emerge... The store offering Witchcraft services and various potions had to be particularly closely inspected; and yet, it was the people that Jenn began to appreciate most.

By the time we had walked past several others also wearing tie-dye, not to mention those in medieval dress, long flowing black capes, or flower adorned hair, Jenn declared:

"These are my people."

She was as content as I'd ever known her to be.

With a very spiritual visit to the fabled Chalice Well, and the iconic Tor completed, it was time to leave. I had a feeling we would be back... the following day if Jenn had anything to do with it...

Perhaps one of the stranger journeys we undertook was just two days after Thanksgiving Thursday.

Jenn was intent on buying a real Christmas tree, it being a tradition among many Americans to have these things in the house the Saturday following Thanksgiving, a good couple of weeks before we Brits tend to think about putting them up.... I therefore faced the difficult challenge of informing Jenn that I doubted she would find a tree this soon as most of the garden centres would not have them out for sale yet.

No... Actually she meant a 'real' tree.... One we could choose ourselves, then chop down and take home with us. I told her, rather matter of fact, that England didn't have Christmas tree 'farms' like they do in America...

Thus, I came home that Friday night to find Jenn dancing around in the hallway, bursting to tell me that, naturally, I was wrong (again)... she had found a Christmas tree farm... and it was a mere ten miles down the road. It would also be opening its doors for the first time this season on Saturday.... tomorrow... at 10am...

We were there twenty minutes early.

The owner was somewhat surprised when he opened the high wooden gates to see two expectant adult children beaming with enthusiasm at the prospect of picking their own tree. It was still November after all.

"Never had that happen before." was all he could say.
We might have been at the January sales, or on a Black Friday mission judging by the way Jenn was hopping from one foot to the other in anticipation as we waited for the owner to trudge back across the car - with only one car in it (ours), open the little kiosk, and select a small paper tag from the shelf.

"What name?" he asked.

"Jenn and Andy" Jenn replied.

"Jenn... and... Andy" he repeated, slowly writing down the same words on the tag.

He handed it to Jenn's outstretched glove.
The instruction was simple. Go find a tree, place the tag on the tree, report back to the office, and then he would go back to the tree with us, cut it down, and the tree would be ours for a price according to its height.

There must have been ten thousand trees in that field but Jenn was determined to find the best one... and before anybody else.... assuming anybody else turned up.
She finally settled on one that was as far away from the kiosk as possible.
Placing the tag on the tree, she then removed her hat and stuck it over the top of the tree... After all, nobody dare remove her hat... I mean, as if anybody else was likely to be there for another week... Then, hand in hand, we ran back to the kiosk.

With tree cut down, bagged, and safely stowed in the car, Jenn formally announced our purchase on Social Media as we sped out of the gate... the car park was now empty.

As a codicil to this story, when we got back home I mounted the tree in its bucket, and between us, we manhandled it into the lounge of our cottage.
Given her excitement, and my general inability to decorate trees, I chose to leave Jenn to adorn it while I made lunch. When I came back into the lounge, I learned just why the tree was so important to her. It was adorned not with the usual shiny plastic trappings so typical of English trees, but with mementoes and decorations she had made and collected over the first years of her life. Christmas then, really was a special time for Jenn... and I was now part of it.

Proposal

Having already been involved in a marriage that lasted far longer than perhaps it should have, I was a man who had no intention of being the marrying kind again. Well that was what I thought anyway...

December arrived. Jenn and I had been living together for just a little over three months. In that time we had laughed and played like children, loved like no other, and been as inseparable as the strongest glue. We could not have been happier. Our world was our own. It was as though we had been born twins she would say; that we had known each other forever, somewhere previously. Life was effortless. We could have been living out of a mud hut, high upon a mountain, and not wanted for a thing. Thus it began to dawn on me that my celibate plans might need reviewing.

And so it was, one rather murky day that I took Jenn to St Nectan's Kieve, a secret place intrinsically linked to Celtic Mythology.
The Kieve lay deep in a wooded valley, almost elven in description, and one heightened by the existence of a waterfall that tumbles over a cliff, through a natural archway, and down into a shallow, darkly quiet, cleft in the rock-face. The overhanging trees, and ledges that lined the cleft, were festooned with ribbons, photographs of the departed, inscribed stones, and personal mementoes.
I led Jenn out onto the stepping stones below the waterfall. We were holding hands and facing each other; time had no meaning.

I gazed into those eyes of hers and they gazed back at me. I had a strange feeling inside; a wondrous but nervous feeling. We stayed there for several minutes, but said nothing to each other.
Slowly, we made our way back to the car and drove home in silence, all the while my mind mulling things over, and wondering, just wondering if Jenn could really be mine. I think she was very much tuned into what was going through my mind too.

Nevertheless, our daily life resumed its happy routine, yet something was different. It was almost as though the subject perhaps neither of us wanted to talk about would, if brought up, lead to discussions of 'too soon', 'we don't know each other well enough', and a dozen other practicalities that perhaps both felt certain might end what we were already fast becoming.

Something broke about two weeks after the visit to the Kieve, and it was me that broke. Barely a hundred days had passed since Jenn had landed at the Airport, but it was enough. I had made a decision.
As usual, I rose early to make coffee and breakfast in bed for my loving Jenn. The previous day had been a particularly wonderful one with her. We had gone out exploring and picnicking in glorious winter sunshine and Jenn had ended it with a superb meal for us, one for which I was refused all access to the kitchen while it was prepared. The evening had been enchanting too; our happiness and the contentment in my heart, beyond all measure.

As I was making Jenn's omelette that morning, I realised that I was at peace for perhaps the first time in my life. I had something that many dream of, but few ever experience.

"A partner who was effortless to be with, who loved me for who and what I was, and one who had set my soul on fire like no other" was how I learned Jenn had later described me. I had had much the same thoughts as I poured her coffee.

I returned to the bedroom, breakfast in hand, but instead of passing the plate and mug to Jenn, I purposefully put them on the bed-side table and sat down on the edge of the bed. Jenn, I think, was expecting something but I had no idea what she thought it would be.

I took her gentle hands, focused on her mesmerising eyes and said simply:

"Will you marry me?"

I had proposed.

The words tumbled out in an almost apologetic way as my mind flashed back to that fateful dinner date request, still less than six months ago.

For a moment I wasn't sure of the answer. I mistook her smile as one perhaps veiled with a sense of endearment. What seemed like forever must have passed in an instant.

She said: "yes".

That was it.

As I went to kiss her though, she pulled away. Puzzled, I pulled back too. She looked meaningfully at her left hand. It was slowly strumming the quilt on the bed, the look on her face, wistful.

A voice inside woke me from my confusion....

"Oh Shit" it cried, I hadn't got a ring!

I disappeared in a rush. I have to believe that Jenn thought I was going to get it from its hiding place. I wasn't. I was scouring our tiny cottage for something vaguely ring-like. After a few minutes of fruitless but noisy searching, to which Jenn later told me she was on the point of coming to see what on earth I was doing to make such a racket, I had a brainwave. Our Christmas ornaments had been secured to the tree with silver ribbon. I remembered that we still had some spare. I grabbed the remaining ribbon, wheeled into the kitchen and set to work fashioning a ring out of it.

Armed with scissors, I paused. I didn't have a clue as to Jenn's ring size. I shrugged and simply wrapped the silver ribbon around my own wedding finger and glued the ends with superglue. If the ring was too large, at least, I hoped, it would be accepted.

Gingerly, and with desperate hope that it was not stuck to my finger, I eased the ring of silver ribbon off my finger and proudly strode into the bedroom.

Jenn was still sat there, waiting.

I took her hand and slipped the silver ribbon over her finger. It fitted perfectly. She raised her fingers to admire my handiwork, and, suitably impressed, launched into a huge and loving kiss.

That evening, Jenn made an internet call to her parents back in America to tell them the news. I can tell you that there is no more surreal experience than asking parents for the hand of their daughter while staring at them on the screen of a laptop. Being that much older than Jenn, I was not expecting the most embracing of responses either. What I got was something of a 'Hell yeah'. It seems that my sweet Jenn had, according to her mother, never been so happy.

And so it was, that plans were laid for our marriage. I cannot even recall how we fixed the date; all I remember was that over the next five weeks, we tackled each step of the process as though they were clues that led to one another.

On my return to work the following Monday, I rang the Recorder's office in order to get the Marriage Licence sorted and the Banns posted; they offered us an appointment at twelve noon... on Christmas Eve. We were to be their last couple before they finished for the holidays.

The following weekend we headed off to find a 'real' engagement ring.

I had some trepidation as I didn't even have a clue about Jenn's spending habits. I need not have worried. Jenn, frugal as ever, picked a simple, understated, but elegant one.

When asked when we would need it, our reply did cause some consternation though. Apparently the chances of it arriving before our intended wedding day, now just four weeks away, were remote they informed us.

When we left the jewellery shop, the significance of what we had just done caused us not a little consternation too … Shit! We had just ordered an Engagement ring… we were planning to get married!

We headed for the nearest beer…

Christmas Eve and our appointment with the Recorder arrived. In a rather stately but dingy office, the jovial official proceeded to go through the same questions he had probably done so hundreds of times before.

For us however, it wasn't so easy to answer them.

"Full names please?"

"So that's what the 'T' stands for punkin"

"Date of Birth please?"

"Errr no, sorry, she means twenty-third of the seventh month. It's an American thing, they put the day and month the other way around. She was not born on the Seventh."

"How did you meet?"

"Well, sort of in a hole in the ground"
(Pause for story)

"When are you planning on getting married?"

"Nineteenth January?"
(Pause for concerned expression on face of Recorder)

"Well let's see if they can fit you in on that day."

"Oh crap, we hadn't thought of that."

And so it went on.

When he finally put the pen down, the Recorder looked at us searchingly. We were sat there still holding hands as we had when we'd walked into his office thirty minutes ago.

He spoke only to inform us that he rarely saw two people so perfectly suited to each other, and for that, he was certain we would have a very happy marriage. Of course, we thought, he probably told every couple that, but no, apparently he didn't...

It was only when we arrived home that we realised we hadn't actually ordered the Wedding rings. It was now mid-afternoon. The country was closed for Christmas.

Jenn though, was still convinced that the tiny family silversmiths business she had found on the Shetland Islands... just as far as it is possible to go to the other end of the country from where we lived, would still be open.

As it turned out, they sort of were... the phone was answered by a kindly soul who confessed to being "only the cleaner", but, nonetheless, he also declared that he was happy to take our order and would see what the silversmiths could do when they came back to work... in January... two weeks' time.... sixteen days before our wedding day.

Christmas and the New Year were spent peacefully together in our own dream; saddened only by the passing of Jenn's Grandmother.

As the news broke, Jenn buried her head in my shoulder and sobbed quietly as we lay on the sofa together.

As I comforted this gentle creature, I knew beyond any doubt in my mind, that I had found the Love of my life... and she was going to be my wife, barely eight months after we had first met.

Mould

As January dawned, there was little sign of wedding nerves from either of us. We had in fact, another pre-occupation...

Our little cottage, we discovered, was riddled with damp. So bad in fact, that a brief technical test showed it was 'off the scale' damp.

In the bedroom, we didn't really need to measure the damp; we could see the tide mark three feet up the wall. Our landlord, no doubt, knew about the problem and had evidently had the place slapped over with a quick coat of paint to hide it, and I, in desperate need of somewhere to live back in sunny, dry, warm August, had fallen for it. Now, in mid-winter, its failings, and mine were all too evident.

After a few arguments with the landlord, it was evident that we needed to find a new place to live, and fast; our precious few possessions were rapidly turning into the same black mould we could watch slowly creeping across the floor.

Having given notice of our intention to quit however, Jenn rightly suspected the landlord would fight to retain our deposit, no doubt so it could be used to repaint the walls before the next unsuspecting couple moved in. Thus, she set about documenting everything... and I mean, everything. Daily mould reports, photographs, and temperature readings were all dutifully recorded in the finest detail. Meanwhile, I called upon my professional contacts... which, being a councillor, and working in the Construction Sector to boot, served only to compliment the defence Jenn was rapidly amassing.

During those last weeks at our now depressive cottage, we spent as little time there as possible. As I went to work so Jenn would make any excuse to do voluntary work at the museum, even if it was for just for a couple of hours. Sometimes she would arrive at my workplace already done for the day, before it was even lunch-time.
When we arrived home those nights, we simply abandoned the cottage and headed for the local Inn, leaving there only when we were in danger of being locked in... although I don't think either of us would have objected to sleeping together on the couch that lay in front of its warming fire... just a couple of convenient steps from the Bar...

When all said and done, there are few things that motivate an Aries male more than the sight of his Leo female in need of a secure roof over her head. Thus, as January marched on towards our wedding date, I was to spend many hours trying to find a new home for us. I must have viewed a dozen or more houses in just one week alone. Yet mindful of my previous effort, and the stand-ard I now had to meet, I couldn't find one. The situation was get-ting desperate.

It was the week of our wedding that my luck finally changed.
I discovered an ultra-modern, detached house, with large airy windows, underfloor heating, and a log burning stove for Jenn to curl up in front of. It didn't have much of a garden area, but there was enough space for a patio table and chairs, room for Maise and Mercedes (our chickens), numerous pot plants... and, most importantly, there was not a hint of mould to be seen, any-where in the house. It's setting in a quiet village, one still remote enough from the civilisation we had no desire to live among, was a bonus... Best of all, we could move in as soon as we wanted to.
I paid the deposit the same day I viewed it and agreed a moving in

date; it was just two weeks after our wedding.

As for the battle to save my deposit from the mouldy cottage - suffice to say that when the Deposit Protection people contacted us about the landlord's claim, Jenn and I submitted a one hundred and fifty page report in response.

... Our deposit was duly returned just a few days later. Apparently the landlord had 'withdrawn' his claim without protest...

I learned that day that, as much as Jenn and I loved our tranquil lives, we were a fearsome team when that tranquility was threatened.

Snow

Our wedding rings arrived on the Wednesday, three days before we were due to be married. Those kindly people in the remote Shetland Islands had not only prioritised their making, but had arranged for them to be flown to Aberdeen for assaying ,and then onward by express delivery to our door. Jenn's conviction about them proved correct.

The following morning, Thursday, Jenn's Engagement ring also arrived. I came home that evening to rather unceremoniously place it on her delicate finger before grabbing our luggage, throwing everything in the car, and heading off to my mother's place some two hundred miles away and the first leg of our circuitous journey to collect her, and then Jenn's mum from London airport, before returning home to Devon just forty-eight hours later.

The next day, with my mother and her luggage now also in the car, we headed for the Airport; Jenn's mother having flown in from America that morning.
It's not every day that you meet your mother-in-law face to face for the first time... in an airport 'Arrivals' lounge... nor every day that two prospective mother-in-law's meet, let alone talk, for the first time there either. Jenn and I hadn't even thought of the potential consequences of that first interaction, but we were on such a crazy wild journey that it hadn't even entered our heads.
As it turned out we need not have worried. There was an instant bond, one, I'd like to think, was swept along by the story Jenn and

I were writing.

With the car now decidedly burdened, we headed home.

Barely an hour into that journey we encountered our first snow-flakes, something a little unexpected. Not more than thirty minutes later those snowflakes had developed into a blizzard. We were now ploughing along a set of tyre tracks cut into the first whiteout I'd seen in a decade.
The snow thickened still further as the traffic begun to queue ahead of us.
We finally ground to a halt.
We were trapped in the middle of Salisbury Plain, an exposed, near treeless plateau in the heart of England, a hundred miles from home... and it was still snowing.

The hours passed by. Jenn had quietly begun to fret that we would miss our date with the Registry Office the following morning. I, was not so quietly contemplating murder towards the asshole who had decided to halt his truck at the top of the hill, just where the two lane highway converged into a single lane. This witless wonder had blocked the entire traffic flow on our side of the road...
If there is such a thing as an omen though, it occurred as we finally crested that hill, a long, long, time later, and paused to look to our right.
There, snow covered, deserted, and set monotone among the white and dark grey of a mid-winter's storm, was Stonehenge, that icon of the English Neolithic age. It was, perhaps, a poignant moment for two lovers whose wedding was to receive a Celtic Blessing.

From that point on, our speed slowly increased as the snow dissi-pated.

There were not inaudible sighs of relief to my announcement that we would make it home by nine that evening. It had taken us almost twelve hours instead of the usual four.

We deposited our respective mothers at our local Inn and scrounged a late meal there before heading home for a fitful night's rest; the significance of the following day almost lost upon us.

Married

Our wedding was at 11am. A quick breakfast, followed by an even quicker change into jeans and tie-dye t-shirt, and we headed out with little more than some warm jackets to fend off the cold and sleet laden rain.

Having collected our mothers from the local Inn, we made our way to the Wedding Venue some twenty miles away.

We arrived early enough, parked the car, and walked off in the direction of the Civil Ceremonies office... except it wasn't where I thought it was.
A fruitless ten minutes searching for signs had rewarded us with no clues at all as to where it might be. With the appointed time fast approaching, and not a soul in sight to ask for directions, I thought it a good, if crazy idea to go and ask the Tourist Information Centre. ... Not a touristy thing to ask I grant you, but I figured that it would be manned by locals who would know this sort of thing... or at least that's what I hoped.

We approached the Enquiry desk, and with several people within eavesdropping distance, announced our plight:

"Excuse me, can you tell me where the Civil Ceremonies Office is please?"

The woman behind the desk smiled and pointed to a door marked

'Civil Ceremony Office'... it was inside the Tourist Information Centre...

We knocked and entered.

A very civilised and formal looking gentleman filled in a few forms, asked us a few questions, took some money from me, and asked us to follow him to another room. To get to it meant going back out into the Tourist Information Centre.

As we crossed the hallway, a quick glance noted several individuals watching us intently. I wondered how many wedding parties they'd seen comprising of two mothers and two oddly matched tie-dye wearing individuals.

We entered the room that had been set aside for the service. It was adorned with a few simple chairs and a plain lightly decorated table. It was here that the Marriage Service was conducted, including the Celtic Wedding Blessing that had been offered to us as though it was some kind of daily special.... buy one Wedding and get a half-price blessing of your choosing.

Nevertheless, since our wedding rings sported a Celtic motif it was only fitting that I had signed up for it.

Now, I have to confess here, that it was not Jenn, but I, a seasoned professional of one prior marriage who forgot his words...

Despite having the ceremony meticulously outlined not ten minutes ago, my brain had something of a mental fart... I gave an emphatic "Yes" instead of the more formal "I Do" to the question of whether I wanted to take Jenn as my lawful wedded wife...

As I spouted out my gaff, there was a pregnant pause.

I turned towards the Official to see him looking at me with a wide eyed 'you bloody idiot' glare.

Mental fart duly expelled, I corrected myself.

A couple of snapshot photographs later and we were handed our Marriage Certificate. As he did so, the official paused to tell us that he rarely saw such a perfectly matched couple. He was certain we would have a very happy marriage. Like the Recorder we'd met just three weeks previously, we thought he told everyone that, but apparently he didn't…

Suitably wed, we headed off to a favoured and ancient Inn Jenn and I had visited on one of our walks.
We entered the virtually empty Bar to find the fire roaring away and a rustic table for four conveniently available in a nearby booth.
I ordered the drinks.
When the barman asked where we'd been, I told him we'd just got married. I'm not sure if he expected an unannounced party of a hundred guests or something but there was a certain look of panic in his eyes.

"How many of you?" he asked cautiously.
"Four." I replied.

I suspect his "The drinks are on the house" response was that of a man grateful that someone somewhere had not screwed up.

Our meal in that cosy little Inn left us with a feeling that we could have stayed there all day, but there were other things to be done, and so we left for home. There would always be more beer and good food at the local Inn that night, for Jenn's mum had seen to it that we had the Bridal Suite… that also meant a night free of mould.
It was a perfect end to what had been a stress free adventure for two people still hurtling along a crazy wonderful path of Love.
As I closed the bedroom door behind us, Jenn turned and said…

"You remember that moment on the beach when you said the seventh wave is always the biggest?"
I nodded.
Jenn smiled…. "That's when I knew."
I closed my eyes and sighed.
The Celt and the Moonbeam had become man and wife.

Status

We moved out of the mould hole and into our new home just a few days later. It didn't take much... a Good Samaritan, a small van, and three trips back and forth was all that was needed. We had even fewer possessions now than when we had begun our lives together. Thus, our new and rather more spacious accommodation looked a little Spartan.

Our enormous bedroom possessed just our bed, two nightstands (not matching), a large blanket box, and a few piles of clothes; while the other two bedrooms remained empty save for my antiquated computer, some piles of books, and a handful of 'I don't know what to do with it' knick-knacks. The lounge at least could lay claim to a hi-fi, a large sofa, and a small fish-tank sat on a coffee table, while the kitchen boasted a washing machine, tumble-dryer, third-hand fridge/freezer, and of course our tiny table and two chairs... with 'slightly chipped' glass candlestick.

Outside, we had artfully positioned our garden table and chairs among our assortment of potted plants while Maise and Mercedes, having inspected their new pen for bugs and grubs; duly noted their approval the following morning with two small brown eggs.

It was at this time though that our happiness was overshadowed by an impending and unmovable requirement for Jenn to return to America to re-apply for the right to live in England as my lawful wedded wife, a status, that we were assured, was not guaranteed ... Agnostic we may have been, but 'God', was evidently alive and well and working for the British Immigration Service.

To make the most of those last few days together, we packed our bags and headed up to my mother's place just sixty-five miles from where Jenn was to depart; our plan to spend what time we had left on the rolling hills and patchwork fields that formed the South Downs, a National Park that can only be described as quintessential England. It was here that Jenn and I always felt most at home.

After spending the night at my mothers' place, and following a tearful goodbye with her, I drove Jenn up to one of the villages that nestled lovingly among those patchwork fields to a gloriously ancient Inn, 'The Fox Goes Free'; a place Jenn had long declared to be her favourite pub. I had booked the Bridal Suite...
We dropped our luggage in our room and headed for the bar. I had already secured the tiny table for two by the roaring fire. It was Jenn's favourite spot.

I don't really remember much of the meal, my eyes were fixed softly on my beautiful wife, her eyes were moist; I could tell by the way they glistened in the flickering light of the fire that she was deeply troubled by the unknown that we about to endure.

As much as I tried to comfort her, and perhaps for the benefit of my own heart too, I knew, and we knew, that our future was beyond our control. All we could do was comply with the myriad complexities of the Immigration service and hope for the best. It angered me intensely that Jenn had to return to America to make that request from there, rather than remain secure in my arms here in her new home, and her new life, but some things in this world offer only misery to those in Love. This was one of them, and there was nothing I could do about it.

We returned to our room.
We lay in each other's arms that night, the tick-tock sound of our lives together slowly running out, keeping us awake.

The following morning, after a lingering breakfast, we drove ever more slowly towards the airport. I meandered through as many lanes and among as many villages as I could on that journey, but our final night in one of the airport's hotels was inevitable.

Jenn checked in her luggage at the airport the following morning and with heavy hearts beating back the tears we said our farewells, feebly assured by the knowledge that we would talk the next day. After all, we had already lived seventy-seven days of our lives on the internet hadn't we? Thus we would be alright doing it again wouldn't we? But we had no idea exactly how many days it would be this time...

I was to learn later that Jenn spent most of her time sobbing in the departure lounge waiting for her plane to an uncertain future. For my part, I drove home in something of a blur; all I remember was that despite the lack of traffic, it seemed to take forever, each mile seemingly taking me further away from the dream that had become my wife.

The following days were spent crammed with every moment we could find in talk, in text, and on video as we finalised Jenn's application and encouraged each other with future plans. Somehow it all had to come good didn't it?

Four agonising weeks were to pass. In all that time we heard nothing other than confirmation the Immigration Service had received, and were 'preparing' Jenn's application for a case worker.

Then, as the fifth week opened, Jenn received a curious email. It was simple enough. It declared that a 'decision had been reached' on her application. The trouble was, we didn't know what it was, and they wouldn't tell us.
With tracking number in hand, we spent the next three days plotting every move that decision made on its way to Jenn's hands. It seemed to take forever.

The day finally dawned with the news that the answer was 'out for delivery' and would arrive with Jenn by 5pm that day. Our nerves, our fears, our excitement, became unbearable as the day crept by.

I was online, talking to Jenn at the time, when I heard the screech of the delivery van. Mid-sentence Jenn simply said "fuck" and flew from my view.

A few moments later I heard her scream.
According to her mother she had snatched the envelope from the delivery driver, torn it open, seen the result, and screamed at the top of her voice before kissing a rather taken aback delivery driver and signing for what she had just torn to shreds. I, of course, was oblivious to all this. My view, staring out of her laptop, was of an empty garden completely oblique to the event that had just taken place.
Thus, thinking the footsteps I could now hear approaching the laptop were Jenn's, I made ready to kiss the screen... her father's face appeared....
It was he who formally advised me that Jenn was coming home.

Jenn's face that night, the warm feeling inside, the tears, the celebratory wine; the pawing at the computer screen; all these things told us that at last, there was to be no more parting.

After almost ten months, the Celt and the Moonbeam were finally to be allowed to live their lives unhindered, together, forever.
When Jenn finally flew into my arms at the airport the following week, we couldn't get out of the place quick enough. Jenn put it succinctly as we fled out the exit:

"I've had enough of airports, too many bad memories."

I nodded wholeheartedly as my hand locked together with hers. This time, I knew EXACTLY where I'd parked the car...

Camping

O ur wedding had been so spontaneous that we hadn't even considered the possibility of wedding gifts. When the subject was finally raised, our Love of the outdoor life made it simple…. camping gear.

The gifts subsequently trickled in and by the time Jenn returned to England in March we had everything we wanted. Jenn added the finishing touch by acquiring a rather space age 'geodome' style tent, one she was particularly proud of.

Thus, it was not long after her arrival home that we felt the urgent need to get out into the wilds and go camping. The trouble was, with all our new, unproven kit, we had no desire to find out what worked and what didn't work in the middle of bad weather… This WAS England, and naturally therefore, weeks were to pass with the forecast precluding any such adventure.

Then, a glimmer of hope arrived one vaguely promising morning.

We chose to head for Dartmoor. It was a place Jenn loved… but it was also a place known for its fickle and often treacherous weather…

The plan though was simple…. We would park the car and walk a few miles to a campground, spend the night there, and the following morning, complete a full circle back to the car. Mindful of the potential for disaster, we chose a location that was not so far away, that if, in the pitch black of night, things didn't work out; a trudge back to the car would not have been difficult. Well, that was the plan anyway.

Thus we set out from the designated car park that morning with little concern.

The forecast though had warned of some 'patchy light drizzle' and sure enough, five minutes into our walk, we encountered said 'light drizzle'. Undeterred, we carried on; we had come prepared for it. Since it was supposed to be 'patchy', we confidently expected it to pass anyhow.

It didn't.

We had covered little more than a couple of miles or so across the moors when that drizzle turned, first to sleet, and then to snow. We faltered. A quick review of the map informed us that we were only about another mile from the campsite so we pressed on. Then the fog descended...

Trying out our new equipment in these conditions was most definitely not part of the plan... and that assumed we could actually find the campsite in what was fast becoming a blizzard. An anxious look at each other and we knew we had to abandon the idea and head home.

I could sense the disappointment in Jenn's face as I walked upstairs to dump the camping gear in one of the spare and still empty bedrooms of our new home.

As I looked around the room though, I had an idea. I began to wonder how absurd it would be to camp in our own home... Realising that our lives were probably quite eccentric anyway, I laid out the groundsheet in the hope that it would fit.

It did.

Returning downstairs to a disappointed Jenn, I beamed at her with one of those childish looks that only children who've just discovered the coolest thing do. I grabbed her hand and led her up the stairs to the room where the groundsheet now lay, and opened the door.

Jenn looked at me, then at the groundsheet, then back at me. I grinned. Having now also discovered the coolest thing, she took to fixing the tent poles together. Soon enough, our tent stood proud on the spare bedroom floor. We then proceeded to roll out our sleeping bags and generally set up camp.

It not being sensible to light our small paraffin stove on the carpeted floor, we headed for the kitchen, and there, while sitting crossed legged on the wooden floor, fired it up.

Jenn opened a packet of the dried food rations we had planned to eat on Dartmoor, and began to prepare it on the little stove... while our built-in cooker, it's entourage of cupboards, and refrigerator full of fresh food, looked on.

We not only cooked our rations on that floor, but sat there and ate them... complete with the plastic plates and cutlery our camping gear also included...

Everything had worked a treat. The tent had gone up in just a couple of minutes, the stove had not only worked perfectly, but proved to be amazingly fast, the cups served the bottle of wine well, and the tent had all the room we needed.

There was one thing we had not been able to practice though... and we were to discover what that was just a couple of weeks later...

When the weather finally delivered the sunny, warm weekend we had been waiting on, we couldn't get out of the house quick enough.

Jenn had already done her homework and found a gorgeous location deep in the heart of Exmoor. It could not have been more perfect.

We arrived to find the main camping fields already busy with camper vans, and at least two large adventure groups. We drove past these as instructed, and found the small field at the far end of the valley that the owners had set aside for the 'quiet' among us.

We chose our pitch, unpacked everything, and with confident ease, erected our space-age tent. We then turned to grab our sleeping bags.

As we spun round, ready to lob them in through the tent's open flap, there was a problem... the tent had gone. A large gust of wind, something not generally found in a Bedroom, had hit the tent like a baseball bat and bowled it clean away across the field.

We learned that moment just what it was we hadn't practiced in the bedroom test... tying a tent down with guy ropes...

We dropped our sleeping bags and chased after it.

As we snared it, some distance across the field, I became conscious of some polite sniggering around us as numerous seasoned British campers looked on at our misfortune. Apparently we were obviously Americans, in part because of our monikered tie-dye t-shirts, but mainly I suspect, because the fully erect tent we were now escorting back across the field, displayed its heritage all rather too clearly on the sides...

Our tent's location, rather too close to the river... something else you don't find in a bedroom, also had a downside we hadn't considered... mosquitoes.

Given how badly we had both reacted to their bites back on Hatteras Island, this was unfortunate, even if they did remind us of how we'd got together.

Jenn spotted the cure.

Dotted around the field were a number of small metal boxes that contained remnants of previous campfires. Reasoning that they were there for our purpose, Jenn lugged an orphaned one back to our tent while I went in search of the 'official' firewood. The resultant fire was all the more pleasing because we had lit it with the tinder kit obtained as yet another wedding gift.

What proved less easy to cure that camping trip was Jenn's ecstatic glee at discovering lambs in the field on the other side of the stream that separated us from them. Those lambs had reached the stage of charging around in groups, springing and bucking their way as only new born lambs full of the joys of spring can. Jenn could not take her eyes off them. I thought for a while she was going to join them.

I learned later that sheep were not commonplace in America.

I knew what I had to do.

A few days later I came home to find that Jenn had already beaten me to it. She was clutching a leaflet that had been pushed into our letterbox. It was one of those 'What's on' newsletters and there, a few inches in front of my face was a headline 'Come and see lambing live'… If I could have missed it, a quivering finger was pointing urgently round the corner of the page at it.

It was a bitterly cold day when we headed for the 'lambing live' farm, but Jenn was not to be denied. The spacious barn was cosy enough though and filled with dozens of expectant ewes and many others already with lambs.

Satisfied with the sight of a few births, we ambled around to the other side of the barn to watch some of the lambs being bottle fed by a group of children. Assuming this was something arranged specifically for families, we made to wander over to the pens of ewes with their own lambs.

We didn't get that far.

As we dragged our eyes away from the bottle-feeding, we almost collided with one of the farmer's daughters. She was holding a lamb.

"Want to hold a lamb?" she said.

In an instant Jenn had thrust everything she was carrying in my general direction.

That moment's photograph confirmed I could not have made her happier.

Curtains

Our Spartan little home had the largest of panoramic windows in every room. Light and airy it certainly was, but what those windows lacked were the curtains that would give us some privacy from the ever passing traffic and pedestrians.

With such accoutrements an expensive project, it was one we hadn't really planned on tackling. Besides which, anyone looking into our home would be disappointed with what they saw; the lounge wasn't exactly filled with expensive artworks, and the dining table possessed only a (slightly chipped) candlestick. We had little fear of finding our home burgled.

To us, the only window of concern was the one in our bedroom, and this only became an apparent need as the days lengthened.
The window faced due east. Thus, the morning sun had a bad habit of blasting its way through that window and onto our bed at stupid o'clock in the morning... despite Jenn's protesting voice telling it to "Fuck off".

The solution was a large black and gold cloth depicting the Celtic 'Tree of Life' that Jenn had brought with her.
If we were being considered the village hippies, we had just confirmed it.

And so it was; our life, the daily routine of newlyweds; as I arrived home from work each evening, Jenn would greet me feverishly as

I would her.

It was during one of those evening embraces, that we were interrupted by a knock at the Kitchen door. It was one of our neighbours. She rejected the invitation from two slightly flushed individuals to come in. Instead, she proffered an armful of curtains. They were purple, perfect choice we thought; they were lined too, and extremely well made. We were overwhelmed by the offer, but at the same time puzzled why anyone would want to give away such beautiful curtains. We made to give her some money, with little or no idea what they must have cost, but she was having none of it. Instead, she told us that the curtains we 'surplus to requirement'; 'a gift'.

We thanked her profusely and she departed, backing away as she left.

When I came home the following night, Jenn had already put them up in the bedroom window.

A few weeks later, as Jenn and I were embracing once again, there was another knock at the door. It was, as Jenn was to call her, 'Curtain Lady'; and once again she was stood there with an armful of beautifully made curtains... the same purple material, the same lining, and, once again, she would not take any money for them, nor come into the house.

Jenn decided to put this set up at the lounge window.

Our Spartan little home may not have had much furniture in it, but it did now have some very fine curtains.

It was not until a few days later that we finally got to chat in any length with 'Curtain Lady' and perhaps thank her more formally. As we did so, it slowly began to dawn on us that our panoramic windows were apparently revealing a lot more than just what a Spartan little home we had...

It also occurred to us we might be able to get a matching set for the kitchen windows too...

Pets

Maise, one of our hens, fell ill.

That day, I arrived home to find Jenn fretting that Maise was not herself. She was not eating and her 'cluck' was 'sort of wrong'. This, I was required to witness.

I deduced that she had probably eaten something she shouldn't have, but offered that she would probably get over it in a day or so.

This was an insufficient response for Jenn, and so, conscience duly prodded, I called the vet.

It being almost six o'clock in the evening, I expected them to be closed.

They weren't.

Five minutes later we are on our way... Jenn with cat-box on her lap containing said chicken.

It is a strange moment indeed to be sat in a waiting room filled with all the usual barks and meows and have a cat-box offer the occasional strangulated 'cluck'....

Following a short diagnosis and armed with the most miniscule of dosages, and an even smaller syringe to drip feed the liquid into Maise's beak, we headed home.

Jenn immediately set up a one bed hospital ward in the kitchen. I had to warn her that Maise was something of a psychotic chicken who would prove to be a difficult patient at best, and one certain to peck and struggle for freedom at every opportunity, potentially causing chaos around the house.

I have a picture to prove that Maise, little more than twenty-four hours later, had become so docile in Jenn's hands, that she would get to enjoy at least one spoon fed meal of scrambled eggs and freshly chopped grass in that hospital ward... the meal neatly served on one of our only two dinner plates...

Supplies of small brown eggs re-commenced three days later.

Not every critter was treated with the same Love and affection by Jenn though.

I was to discover this one evening when Jenn, on suddenly recoiling her feet onto the sofa, screamed:

"What the fuck is that?" as she pointed towards a sizable English House spider scuttling across the floor.

Having lived with these all my life, I merely replied that it was harmless, despite its near four inch diameter.

Dissatisfied with my response; Jenn commanded her pet cat Arwen to kill it.

'Arwen' looked at the spider, then at Jenn and back at the spider. I could tell that her response was along the lines of "not bloody likely."

She remained unmoved.

In the end it was up to me to deal with said spider.

A few days later I came home to the sound of something being hit with what sounded like a hammer. I assumed Jenn was hanging pictures...

No, she was actually beating the crap out of an already very dead House spider with the sole of one of her wooden shoes...

Arwen sat by and taking notes that day, eventually took up the challenge when she found that if she played her cards right, these house spiders could occupy her for half an hour or more, depending on how long it took for their legs to fall off under the onslaught of her paws. As the last leg stopped wriggling, Arwen would consider it safe to crunch up the remains... leaving me to account for all the legs...

However, there was one pet Jenn would become besotted with...
We were visiting a pet store one day for the usual sack of bird seed when Jenn spotted an area of the store given over to orphaned 'critters' in need of re-homing.
Among them was a hamster, which of course, knew exactly how to stand up on its stubby little hind legs and put on a face pleading for a new home.
As Jenn pulled herself away from his beady little eyes and wandered off to find cat food, I discretely made enquiries. I had to, I knew Jenn adored him, and besides, I could not have handled the guilt of leaving him there to ply his trade on another unsuspecting human.

Ten pounds is the going rate apparently for an orphaned hamster, complete with cage, toys, a month's supply of food, about a year's supply of yogurt drops ...and a Certificate of Ownership for Jenn.

There was now a new man in her life. As much as I would do anything for Jenn, so she would do anything for the now named 'Fernworthy'... one very human, and, as we were to discover, cerebrally advanced hamster who possessed an unerring ability to extract more than his prescribed daily ration of yogurt drops from his doting humans.

I'm not entirely certain as to who had the idea of building Fernworthy a penthouse suite either, but I came home one night to find he had got one. Jenn had evidently also been asked if she could cook up some haute cuisine hamster food for him...
Ours would be down the pub that night as Jenn hadn't realised the time...

Food

J enn and I knew a great deal about what each other liked to eat, we had discussed much of that during those long days and nights of constant Internet chatter. Cultural differences in cuisine were therefore to be part of our exploration of life together.

As I would make Shepherd's pie, so Jenn would respond with her Southern Chicken and Dumplings. Of course, there was also to be the occasional 'lost in translation' moment too...

I happen to like Macaroni Cheese, but when Jenn offered to make what she called 'Mac n' cheese' one day, it was not until it arrived on the table that I realised 'Mac' was in fact short for Macaroni. Yes, it was the same dish.

It was not long either before we discovered that, as we were a seamless team in Love and life, so we would be in the preparation of meals together.

During a visit from Jenn's mother we decided to attempt making Moussaka.

This is a complex dish at best, and yet, as I set about making the ragu, so Jenn took to slicing the eggplant and potato and frying them off without instruction. As I then set about laying the ragu and fried slices into the oven dish, so Jenn would set to work on the roux and sauce. By the time the sauce was ready, naturally I had already grated the cheese for the topping. It was as though we had worked together and practiced our art for years. The resulting dish though took far less time to demolish than it did to cook...

Cooking and foody things were not always to be this smooth though...
I am not, nor ever have been, fond of hot spicy dishes. Jenn found this out one day when she prepared an Indian curry.

We had shopped together as usual, so when I saw the jar of curry go into the basket I thought no more than 'ah yes, curry.... good choice'. What I didn't notice until I put a spoonful of the finished result into my mouth that night was that Jenn had picked up 'Hot Madras'... hot by most definitions, burning holes in the soles of my shoes by my definition.

Initially I said nothing; I so did not want to disappoint her. My laboured rate of consumption must have given Jenn a clue that I was not overly enjoying it, but I think it was the perspiration that started to bead on my forehead that finally gave the game away. Her response was immediate:

"Oh god I've melted my punkin!"

She rushed to the kitchen sink and returned with a large glass of water. I gulped enthusiastically. I was disappointed that I had failed to hide my discomfort, and finally had to admit defeat on her lovingly prepared curry. I felt compelled to make amends... and I knew exactly what to do.

Jenn had a Love of hot chillies, far hotter than I thought rational. Thus, when I saw a leaflet encouraging visitors to try the hottest chilli in the world at a local chilli farm, I could not miss the opportunity to challenge her taste buds.

We walked into the Chilli farm shop that weekend to find they had given over one whole side of it to an impressive display of chillies, each complete with its own samples of sauces, with and without seeds, all conveniently arranged from mildest to hottest; the further you progressed down the display the redder the backdrop to the display got.

Jenn headed straight past the Habaneros and made for the last one in the line... it had a warning sign hanging overhead and a backdrop of raging flames.

She took a spoonful of the seeded version...

Out of the corner of my eye I watched some very nervous staff move as though a well-rehearsed 'crash team'. As one grabbed a large tub of ice-cream, so the other lunged for a jug of iced water and spittoon.

In a somewhat blasé way I told them not to worry; we were witnessing a potential world champion fire-eater who, as she swallowed the seeds of the hottest chilli in the world, simply said:

"Nice"

As the crash team stood by in silent amazement, I helped myself to the spoonful of ice-cream that was poised halfway to Jenn's mouth, mumbled "thanks", and stood back while Jenn explained her love of Chillies, was a 'southern' thing.

As if to endorse Jenn's fire-eating ability, when we stopped for a bite to eat on the way home, she took to pouring lashings of the oil dressing labelled 'Danger - Hot' onto her Pizza... much to the concern of the chef who promptly reminded her of the label. As Jenn licked the oil from her finger, I turned to him and said:

"It's a southern thing."

Beds

J enn had determined we needed a headboard for our bed...
Being the frugal type, we soon discovered that these things
are rarely cheap, and, for the most part, pink, or just twee.
There was only one thing for it. We'd make one ourselves...

Thus, armed with a few measurements we headed to the nearest hardware store to search for the wood that would make the
frame.
The prepared lengths for the uprights were easy enough to find,
but when it came to the material for the head-board itself, this
proved to be ridiculously expensive. Jenn was having nothing of
it.

Seeing that the store had one of those large industrial cutting
machines for custom orders, I wandered over and asked the bored
operator what they did with the offcuts. A nearby rack of forlorn
odd-shaped pieces provided the answer.
I didn't have much hope of finding what we needed, but, as luck
would have it, there, lurking at the back of the rack, was the ideal
piece. It just needed one side trimming off and it would be perfect. The operator said he would be happy to oblige for a cash
offer. My cash offer was Five pounds ... including cutting.
He accepted.

To find the right material to cover the headboard with, I took
Jenn to one of those mysterious old family-owned shops that
sold that sort of thing. You know the type... the ones where the

staff have worked there for forty years and, having never found their way out from among the randomly stacked piles of material, were still time-bound to the dress-style of the day they'd first started work there. We headed for the shop's darkest recesses.

Sure enough, there it was... a gaudy, plush looking roll of cloth, with a large label pleading 'Buy me. (Please)'
We unravelled the material to get a better look. The design revealed gaudy shades of green and gold. It was perfect.... even if it did look as though it had been ordered for the store opening. What was more, there was just enough left for what we needed.
After converting the price from guineas and groats to pounds and shillings and then onto dollars, Jenn was satisfied that with the money saved from the bargain offcuts at the hardware store, we could afford it.

Back home, the project was started immediately and it was not long before I had measured, drilled, and checked the frame would fit the bed. Jenn then set to work cutting and wrapping the board with the material. As she held it in place so I tacked it onto the board. Somewhat less than two hours after we had started, there it was, our gaudy, certainly unique, and to be much loved, headboard.
Jenn looked at me with a little wonder.

"We made a headboard punkin" she said.

I returned her smile. I felt not a little proud that it had gone so effortlessly for I was not the best handyman, and in designing and making the headboard, had ventured into what I saw as a daunting, never before tried, test of my practical skills.
It was time to celebrate...

Sometime later, and with Jenn's mother coming to visit us, we realised we needed a bed for the guest room – the one we had used for our camping adventure.
Jenn found what she wanted and duly ordered it for delivery. It

was due the week her mum arrived.

Delivery day came… not with a bed, but with a phone-call to say that the bed was out of stock and they had made a mistake selling it to us.
Jenn was livid, but rather than simply throw a paddy and achieve nothing (generally my approach…), she articulated the caller into conceding that they had to offer an alternative for delivery in the next forty-eight hours… and at the same price… regardless of the fact that every 'alternative' was at least a third more expensive…
The deal done, all we had to do was collect it from the local store, along with a suitable mattress and some linen. We headed down there the following day.

Now, there are days when a store offers some amazingly good deals, but today was exceptional. I still don't quite know how Jenn did it, but, with a special offer on mattresses if you bought a bed at the same time, a voucher Jenn had acquired to cover the extra cost of the bed over and above what she had already paid, and a further special offer on linen if you brought a mattress… the still puzzled shop assistant opened the cash register and handed Jenn thirty-five pounds…

I learned that day to let Jenn do all future financial negotiations.

Digging

J enn told me of a long standing promise she had made to assist on an archaeological field school back in America. She would be gone five, perhaps six weeks.

Still so nervous of our perceived vulnerability to the Immigration people, it was not surprising that she wasn't entirely looking forward to it. It also meant another separation for us to endure, albeit one softened by the knowledge that I would be able to join her for a week while she carried out her duties.

Thus, two weeks into Jenn's absence, and not foregoing the nightly updates from across the Atlantic, I flew into Charleston to join her.

Jenn of course, was there to greet me, and naturally our terrible parting of a mere two weeks ago was lost in a Heathcliff and Cathy moment as we collided in the middle of the airport lounge.

Hands firmly locked together once more, and with a colleague of Jenn's acting as chauffeur, we headed back to the apartment where I was to spend a week sharing a room with Jenn as husband and wife.

That short-lived week was an enjoyable one, our time together being both private and as an object of interest for those working around us. We didn't mind the latter; our lives and the Love story we were writing had been pretty much public from the start... and it still was...

When Jenn finally returned to England, I was, as always, there to greet her. Airports were not our favourite places and we didn't stay long enough for anyone to raise a questioning finger at us, even though Jenn's now legal and formal approval to be in England as my wife was beyond questionable doubt.

She had been back just a couple of weeks when her phone rang to inform her that she was now to get her first official contract as an Archaeologist in England. It was another short five week affair, but it was work, paid work. There was just one snag...the site was over a hundred miles away, and somehow Jenn had to meet her transport to site at a rendezvous point thirty miles from our house... at a little after six in the morning... every morning.

Being something of a logistical brain, I came up with a plan. It would mean a very long day for both of us, but it was a small sacrifice for Jenn's future.
Each morning we would rise at 5am. There would follow a short bedlam in the bathroom before we headed for the kitchen and a rushed breakfast and packing of lunches. Everything Jenn needed for her archaeology would already be packed and propped against the kitchen door.
With plates washed and dried, and Jenn's coffee carefully transferred to her flask, we would set off on the drive to the rendezvous point.

Those morning drives were never tedious, there being so little traffic on the road, save for the odd deer, and myriad number of rabbits playing 'chicken'... that we would invariably arrive early. We would then sit and chat away the wait until her transport arrived. Our parting was a longing kiss, a squeeze of the hands and a few words of encouragement. I would watch as she set off and then drive back past our home, and onward to my place of work.

As my working day finished, I would race home, change clothes, prepare something for dinner, jump in the car and hurtle back down past the deer and rabbits still trying to beat me at 'chicken';

and onwards to the rendezvous point.

My Jenn, now suitable covered in the grime and dirt of her archae-ological passion would jump in the car, and we would once more head home.

The chatter those evenings was that of two people who had not seen each other for months...

As soon as we arrived home, Jenn would prepare her kit bag for the following day and then head for the shower while I finished making dinner; Jenn after all, nearly always had something ready for me when I came home from work... I didn't need any prompt-ing to do the same for her.

Bedtime came early those five weeks.

Jenn's Love of archaeology was such that she never truly switched off from it...

Each time we took off for a walk somewhere, it only required the faintest glint from the tiniest piece of broken pottery or por-celain half buried in the ground to stop her in her tracks, stoop down, prize it from the earth with whatever she had to hand, and scrutinise it. Satisfied that its context did not suggest there was an undiscovered ceramics factory or, as in the case of a piece of Roman roof tile she found one day while walking the South Downs, an unknown Roman Villa, she would carefully remove it to her rucksack for later cleaning, closer examination, and 'filing' on the kitchen windowsill. Well, kitchen windowsill for about the first month... the lounge windowsill and our bedroom win-dowsill soon became extensions to her rapidly growing museum.

Occasionally, those tiny fragments would bring her to her knees, especially if the fragment had a companion. On one occasion, we stumbled upon a disused quarry which had evidently been used as the local rubbish dump for some considerable time. Within minutes, Jenn had collected two dozen or more pieces of porcel-ain and clay pipe stem.

As she continued feverishly combing back the earth, it was left to me to smile benignly at passers-by as their faces revealed at first surprise, then puzzlement, and finally 'should they be doing that?' looks.

"It's OK, she's an archaeologist" was all I could think to say at that point, but I was never sure that Jenn's improvised twig looked compelling enough to be thought of as an item in an archaeologist's toolkit...

After about twenty minutes of digging, Jenn stood up and declared that the dump was probably last used about a hundred years ago.

As she wandered off with the usual "come on punkin", I looked back and wondered if we should cover our tracks... she had scrapped back several square feet of topsoil.
Reasoning that the disturbance could be put down to a badger... or perhaps several dozen badgers, I hurried to join her.

Peas

I 've never had the best of luck with cars, and Jenn was to find this out fairly quickly.

I had a pretty decent car when she first met me, but it had a built-in ability to break down or fall sick with routine monotony. One morning, while we were still at the mouldy cottage, it was the starter motor.

Luckily, having had so many previous experiences of being towed, and/or having to trudge miles to find help, I'd learned that breakdown insurance was essential... especially if Jenn was not to suffer the same fate should she ever borrow the car to go somewhere.

The policy was officially a 'get you home' arrangement, but on the morning of the Starter Motor failure I managed to persuade the operator that my car was more than the required half mile from my front door... Well it was... almost... OK it was actually about 800 yards short of that target, but thankfully, our little home was so remote that the operator had absolutely no idea that the description I gave for our 'breakdown' location was actually the allotted parking space for our house... in a field about a hundred yards from our front door.

The engineer who answered our call though had his suspicions... especially when Jenn offered him a cup of tea...

Whatever he must have thought, he decided to take pity on the two childlike individuals, dressed in tie-dye and holding hands that were stood anxiously waiting on his opinion.

Yup, the starter motor had given up, burnt out in fact.

Following Jenn's perfect crestfallen pout, he elected to get our car going so we could drive to town and purchase a new one.

We arrived at the car parts store without further incident.

I left Jenn in the car, engine running, with specific instructions not to touch anything... (I told you we were kids), while I secured the replacement starter motor.

When we arrived back home, it was still early enough for us to go somewhere for the day, so, despite the bitter cold, I manned up and crawled under the car to remove the defective motor. Yes, like all cars, mine was designed to ensure that things likely to fail were in the most inaccessible place... Nevertheless, I was learning to be grateful for Jenn's 'Redneck's daughter' background. When my voice from under the car proffered an outstretched hand pleading for a sixteen millimetre open-ended spanner, that's exactly what it got.

Car fixed, we headed off as though nothing was to spoil the day.

A few weeks later, it was service time for my reliably unreliable drive.

My friendly garage owner, one of those people for whom nothing was too much trouble, always had a spare car ready for me... he knew full well there were bound to be various bits that would need to be ordered and furthermore that they would take several weeks to arrive.

These spare cars though, were usually of dubious parentage, and the smallest of their ilk. Quite where he got them from I didn't want to ask. His only advice was to not drive them too far... or too fast...

Thus it was that when I arrived home that night, Jenn came out of our cottage to find me sat in what she described as a 'Green pea'.

At heart I think she loved its feisty appeal, especially when, with foot to the floor, it would game-fully do everything it could to fly.

The 'Green Pea' stayed with us for two weeks, only to return, much to Jenn's delight, when my car limped once more to the garage just three weeks later.

Things didn't get much better after we had moved to our new home. In fact, such were the problems I was having with my car that I decided I would hire one for our impending holiday rather than risk spoiling it with another breakdown.

"I want something small and economical." I said to the hire car agent.

What I got was something called a 'Spirit' which was soon to become the 'spit' and eventually the 'zit'... for it was about that size and just as painful.
Jenn though was ecstatic...

"Blue pea! Blue pea!" she cried as I led her to see it.

It was quite an experience to drive too, being nothing short of a gutless wonder. As we drove uphill, any hill, both of us would spontaneously start to rock back and forth (as you do), in the vague hope that such action would help the 'zit' to make it to the top.

For a while thereafter, my car behaved itself, but only for a while. Just as life appeared to be returning to normal, a light on the dashboard had me scuttling for the driver's handbook only to discover those immortal words 'take the vehicle to a dealer as soon as possible'.

Sure enough, I was to return home with another car of dubious parentage, and this one had a unique problem... the exhaust was blowing; well actually, it was mostly missing.
When Jenn and I went out in what she immediately christened as the 'Yellow pea', conversation was impossible ... the absurdity of

trying to do so simply resulted in hysterical laughter ... and dropping down a gear in order to pass someone was a mischievous necessity, not least to see if we could terrorise the other driver into thinking we had modified the engine for drag racing.

The day finally came when I was no longer prepared to spend money on yet another ludicrously expensive part for my car.

Being a little cash-strapped at the time, I asked Mr friendly garage owner if he knew of anything that might be cheap and reliable. As a matter of fact he did... he offered to sell us one of his hire cars.

I collected it from the garage one Friday afternoon and drove home, my mind filled with the vivid expectation of Jenn's response.
I duly got it...
She opened the kitchen door, and, with me still sat in the driver's seat, skipped around the car shouting:

"Red pea! Red pea!"

Bread

We had celebrated our second Christmas together. Yes, the Christmas tree farm had remembered us from the previous year... and January welcomed our first wedding anniversary.

As March arrived, we were now looking forward to longer days and getting out more... our camping gear demanded it. I had in fact already planned a weekend away on our beloved South Downs. It was to be a preparatory hike for future long distance events... Jenn was getting excited; it was just three weeks away.

Meanwhile, she had been doing some planning of her own. She had spent two days perfecting a loaf of bread. It was no ordinary loaf but one designed to win a competition for a romantic meal for two at a local restaurant.

Thus, on the morning of the competition, with said loaf in hand, we drove to town, parked our car, and headed for the market where the judging was to be held.

Loaf duly registered and very carefully positioned on the table, we wandered off to nose around and of course to say 'Hi' to the many people we knew there.

Then, just as judging hour approached, Jenn's hand slipped from mine. Something was wrong. I looked searchingly at her as her eyes glazed over and she sagged to a nearby bench. I knelt down by her and tried to focus her eyes on me. I couldn't. Something was badly wrong. The alarm bells were ringing inside. I called for help.

The paramedics were there in just a couple of minutes.
I was asked all the obvious questions: "Was Jenn pregnant?" "Has this happened before?" My urgent "No" and a few quick checks was enough for them to call an ambulance.
For reasons peculiar, I could not go with Jenn in the ambulance. Thus, as she left the scene, I ran to the car and tore down the road to the hospital.

Jenn was already in the emergency room when I arrived and the medics had already ruled out all the usual possibilities.
For the next few minutes, I sat by her side holding her hand, trying desperately to re-assure her things would be alright, but Jenn was fighting her own battle, with, I knew not what.
Suddenly she sat upright, her fought for words simple enough...

"Don't give Fernworthy too many yogurt drops."
And with that, Jenn simply lay back down and closed her eyes.

"I won't" was my faltering reply... my mind too focused and confused by what was happening before my eyes to understand the significance of what she had said.
I screamed loudly for help.
Within seconds, Jenn was on her way for a CT scan. I was not allowed to follow.

The wait seemed forever but could not have been more than a few minutes before a white coat entered our cubicle; Jenn was nowhere to be seen.
He slowly sat down opposite me. His movements grave enough for me to know the news was not good.

"Jenn's suffered a significant Brain Haemorrhage."

The words were slow to sink in.

"We are preparing her for an airlift to a specialist neurological unit. You can see her now, but only for a minute, it's pretty busy in there. We have placed her under heavy sedation. She cannot respond."

He led me into a nearby room. As I walked in, my eyes were filled with the sight of my dear Jenn. She was in a deep sleep and surrounded by more technology and medical staff than I thought possible, and they were frenetic in what they were doing for her. For a moment, they parted so I could kiss my beloved wife's forehead and mutter something about it being OK, that I wasn't going anywhere, and that I loved her.
As I was gently ushered back from her side, the air ambulance crew arrived to whisk her away.

I drove back to our little home in something of a daze. I had no idea what to do. For some reason my mind settled on gathering some things I thought Jenn might need. It was all rather logical, but so illogical.

As I prepared to leave, Arwen, Jenn's beloved cat looked pensively down the stairs at me. I told her that her 'mummy' was ill and that I might be some time. I topped up her water and food, closed the kitchen door behind me and headed down the road at breakneck speed.

Seventy miles later I raced into the reception area for the neurosurgery unit, heart pounding.

"Was Jenn OK? Was she going to make it?" was all I could think to ask.

I wasn't sure what to make of the looks I got, but they were silent. One of the surgeons slowly walked over to me and guided me to a small room. He said nothing and left.

I slowly sat down and prepared myself for news that Jenn had suffered a life-changing event; something that could take years to recover from, perhaps something she might never fully recover from.

Inside, I clung to that belief and the conviction that I would be by her bedside, talking to her, watching over her, and doing what devotions I could for her, forever... if that was what it was going to take. She was my wife, and much the better half of my soul.

A few anxious minutes later, a man I took to be the surgeon, and a smartly dressed woman walked into the room and sat down opposite me. They spoke quietly.

"Jenn has suffered a massive subarachnoid haemorrhage. When she arrived here, there was nothing we could do. Jenn died three minutes into the flight."

There was silence.
I looked back and forth between them. I almost didn't hear the last words.

Then it began to sink in.
The word 'No' began issuing from my mouth over and over again. As the denial grew louder, the tears began to flood down my cheeks. My heart plunged from my chest as the convulsions of unbridled grief left my lungs empty, and my mouth open for air it could not breathe.

Her world, our world, had ended, and the gorgeous creature, my angel, my Moonbeam; my wife, a woman so at peace with her world that to be part of it was to live in a place of magic, was gone...

After some while alone, I was led to see Jenn. She had been placed in a quiet room of subdued lighting. As the vision unfurled before me, I broke down again, quieter this time, but with eyes firmly focused on her face; it was perfect, and it was at peace.

They found me a chair into which I slumped. I was as close to Jenn as I could be. Minutes later, my phone rang.... Jenn had won the romantic meal for two at the restaurant... Words failed me. I ended the call.

Perhaps an hour later, the question of whether Jenn was a Donor was gently broached. A little fazed by the request, it took me a moment to realise why they were asking me. Of course, I was Jenn's next of kin.
I had no idea. These are not the things one talks about when in Love. Her mother might know, I mumbled, but then had to explain she was on a plane somewhere over the Atlantic, and it would be another twenty-four hours before she was likely to arrive at the hospital.

There was so much more that happened that night... yet I can remember only the appearance of compassionate support, the ignored advice to eat or drink something, and the gentle, almost reverential checks made on Jenn's comfort by the ever attendant nurses.

Sometime in the middle of that night, it was confirmed that Jenn was a registered donor, in America. Her wishes had no legal jurisdiction here in England, however, but I could not deny Jenn her wishes.
I agreed to sign what I needed to so they could be carried out, but on condition that her mother could see her daughter first.
It seemed the right thing to do.
Throughout that long night, I never left Jenn's side. I stayed there unfailingly, there was no other place to go, and there was no other place I wanted to be. The tears never stopped falling.
The following morning, Jenn's mother arrived, far earlier than it should have been possible for her to be there; her story of a prioritised landing, and emergency dash with a police escort, one to be told in its own right.

And thus, a short while later, I kissed my beloved Jenn on the forehead, and said simply:

"Goodbye Moonbeam. I Love you. I always will."

It was time to go.
Jenn would live on in others I told myself, and I knew she would live on in my heart, forever.

There followed that strange time when family gathers, affairs are straightened out, and services are held.

When the quiet finally descended upon that empty little house of ours, the laughter and warmth no longer present, I lit the candle in our (slightly chipped) candlestick, lay down on our forever shared sofa, and with Jenn's ashes in my arms, cried myself to sleep.

Morning no longer had a purpose.

Epilogue

A few days later, as I opened the refrigerator, my eyes focused on a scrap of paper stuck to the door. It was a list of all the things Jenn and I had planned to do. Top of the list was our weekend trek across the South Downs.

No-one will ever know or understand how hard it was to walk along those southern hills that weekend.
I carried Jenn's ashes with me. They were safe in my, our, backpack; my hand though, was empty.
When I stopped to rest, I could only imagine her laying there with me among the fields of barley, the poppies, the cornflowers; safe in my arms. She would have been gazing into my eyes as mine would have been fixated on hers; while the picnic I know she would have so lovingly and excitedly prepared, would have been spread out around us.

I talked to her the whole time I made that walk.
The tears flowed as I laboured up the highest hills. At times, I almost wished I would be found, stilled by the side of the path, my hand reaching out for hers. But no, I was to make that journey no matter the times I simply wanted to sag to my knees, done with life.

As I approached the campsite of our planned overnight stay, I passed through a field full of gambolling lambs; the tears flowed once again, as they would that night while I pitched our tent, alone, among the crowded but empty paddock.

As darkness fell, I remember sitting outside our tent and purposefully lighting a candle on the little shrine Jenn had made for us, then lying back to gaze up at the millions of stars above, just as we had done so the night of our first kiss, and on so many times since. Perhaps she was OK somewhere. Perhaps she was watching over me. Perhaps she was one of those bright stars I could see... somewhere up there. Maybe one of them was tie-dyed. I hoped so.

The following day, I reached the train station at the end of the walk and sat down in silence on the empty platform. There was no cheering voice declaring "We made it punkin." No hug, no lingering kiss, and no heart-warming smile to gaze upon; but there was something else... I had begun to walk the path we had planned to walk together, and somehow deep in my heart, it felt as though my sweet Moonbeam had been there all the time.

She still is.
I know this, for I am the Celt...

Silent Dream

A cadence of chimes plays the sound of Love.
among the carefree haze of summer fields.
While poppies tickled by the wind do play,
a lark above, sings the barley hay.

I spy a blue dress twirling, swaying,
enchanting smile, the gold of our day.
My heart so happy this fleeting hour,
as memory shines upon a sweet Sunflower.

For all the clouds and strife life brings,
I care not for the wind, or tears of the rain.
For I sleep in the warmth of a silent dream,
as I lay in that field, with my dear Moonbeam

Adventures Of A Middle-Aged Fart

Laugh out loud, occasionally gasp, or simply pity the antics of the author as he toils up mountains (and occasionally falls down them), perspires and curses his way across the south of France, becomes a sailor (even though he can't swim), narrowly avoids plunging over a cliff edge (several times), haggles his way (badly) across Morocco, buys chocolate from a Kalashnikov wielding Serbian, and escapes from drug-crazed bovines in Montenegro before finally witnessing a Class Action lawsuit against a tree in America... Your adventure starts here.

Richard Grenville And The Lost Colony Of Roanoke

England's ill-fated first attempt to colonize America at Roanoke Island in 1587, has been the focus of numerous studies, fictional re-tellings, and media interpretations. From his unique position as former Mayor of Bideford, the English town so intrinsic to the story, Gabriel-Powell conducts a thorough re-examination of the story. Join the author as he re-interprets original transcriptions, and draws light from newly discovered documents and archaeological evidence, to conclude that some of those colonists may have survived long enough to leave descendants who walk upon American soil today.

Made in the USA
Middletown, DE
20 April 2022

64566277R00068